ANNIE'S ATTIC MYSTERIES ®

The Legend *of* Fuller's Island

Jan Fields

Annie's ®
AnniesFiction.com

Library of Congress-in-Publication Data
The Legend of Fuller's Island / by Jan Fields
p. cm.
I. Title
                    2012912100

AnniesFiction.com
800-282-6643
Annie's Attic Mysteries®
Series Editors: Ken and Janice Tate
Series Creator: Stenhouse & Associates, Ridgefield, Connecticut

10 11 12 13 14 | Printed in China | 9 8 7 6 5

Matthew Steven Fuller was hardly a man given to su-
perstition or gossip. Even into his eighties, he stood ramrod
straight with eyes as bright and piercing as a hawk. He wore
a beard, well tended, but concealing. I never remember see-
ing him smile, though I never saw him lose his temper either.
He was like a firm pillar that you knew would stand forever. I
could think of no man less likely to die from a curse or the bite
of a demon hound, and yet, no other answer has appeared,
even these many years after the event.

> The Fuller Family History
> *By Steven Fuller*
> *Private printing, 1925*

As Annie Dawson turned the yellowed page, she
caught the sharp scent of old book, a smell
mixing leather, old ink, and probably more than a little
mildew. She brought the book closer to her nose to squint
at the notes written in the margins. Each one reflected the
unique wit of her grandfather. For Charles Holden, reading always had been an interactive experience. He read the
author's words, and then added his own in little notes and
drawings along the margins. When Annie found a stash of
her grandfather's books in the attic, she'd brought them
down and began reading them, mostly for the pleasure of

hearing her grandfather's voice in the penciled words.

Sitting in Grey Gables, the house Gram and Grandpa had shared, Annie had often felt her grandmother's love as she had restored the house and unearthed her grandmoth-er's treasures from the attic. Now, through the books, she was having the same sense of her grandfather's love and delightful perspective on life.

Luckily, she'd begun her reading with one of Grand-pa's more unusual books, a rather fanciful family his-tory he'd collected somewhere. At least, it was titled as a family history, though it read more like a cross between a memoir and a ghost story. From his comments, clearly her grandfather had found parts of the book as outrageous as Annie did. Still, it was fun to read the juxtaposition of the author's long-winded and slightly pompous prose and her grandfather's quick-witted responses.

As she laughed aloud at some of her grandfather's hu-morous notes, a project idea began forming in her mind. She would collect some of the cleverest of her grandfa-ther's sayings from margin notes in his books. Then she could sprinkle them among anecdotes about his work and family from his journals. She had piles and piles of his books and journals as source material. She would have a few copies bound as presents for the family—*Quotes From Grandpa Charles*. It would offer a sense of his wonderful personality to generations who never had the blessing of knowing him.

Annie sat back, thinking. Her grandchildren, Joanna and John, never met their great-grandfather. They had no real memories of their great-grandmother either, though at least Betsy Holden had gotten to see them when they were babies. It was still hard to believe that Gram had been gone for several years now— some days, the loss of her grandmother still felt sharp in Annie's heart.

She sighed and turned her attention back to the book.

A chubby gray cat lay at the end of the sofa, curled up in a mildly disgruntled pile. Boots, like Grey Gables, was Betsy's before she was Annie's, and Boots never liked it when Annie sat on the sofa with her legs tucked under her, since it left no room for a cat to pile up in her lap. Suddenly, Boots sat up straight, her nose pointed toward the front door.

"Did you hear something?" Annie asked.

Boots never moved a muscle. She just continued with the fierce frozen stare that cats are so good at, as if she could see into another dimension where things were far more exciting.

Annie shifted on the sofa, putting her feet on the floor and feeling for her shoes. She slipped into them just as she heard footsteps on the porch. She was halfway across the room by the first knock. When Annie opened the door, she found her best friend, Alice Mac-Farlane, picking a piece of autumn leaf from her thick auburn hair. The spots of gold and red on the blown leaf were an almost perfect match to the gold and red of Alice's twill jacket.

Grinning at Annie, Alice took a step away from the door and gestured with a flourish toward the silver-haired man leaning heavily on a wooden cane behind her.

"Jim Parker!" Annie said, stepping forward to give the smiling man a hug. "I didn't know you were coming for a visit!"

"It was a bit impromptu," Jim said, his voice warm and gravelly. He hugged Annie with one arm, while keeping a firm grip on the sturdy cane in the other. "I've hit a snag with my latest book and thought I would come and visit my gorgeous muse." He cast a mischievous look toward Alice.

"He knows I'm very susceptible to flattery," Alice said.

"Well, come in and tell me about your snag," Annie said. "I'm not a muse, but I'd still like to hear what you've been up to."

Jim laughed and shook his head. "Miss Annie, I would never consider calling you my muse," he said. "I expect that after Alice finished roughing me up, your mayor friend would have a go. I know from experience that he can be a bit hot-tempered."

Jim walked through the door with a slightly uneven gait from his prosthetic legs. A photographer, he had lost both of them when he was a war correspondent and an explosion had brought down the hotel where journalists were staying in Kosovo.

Annie felt her cheeks warm at Jim's mention of Ian Butler. Her relationship with the handsome mayor was complicated. They were good friends, but they both were beginning to suspect it might be growing into more.

Alice gave Jim a playful poke. "Just so you know who you'd have to face *first*."

Jim caught her hand in his and gave it a squeeze. "You're always first with me." Then he turned back to Annie. "So, how's your gallant mayor doing?"

"You didn't stop by his office to visit?" Annie asked, her voice teasing, as she led them into the foyer.

Jim burst into laughter. "You know, I do believe I was growing on him a little the last time I was in town, but that still doesn't mean I want to push my luck. There's been a time or two when I half-expected him to take a swing at me."

"I'm sure Ian wouldn't go around brawling," Annie said, though she had to admit inside that she suspected he'd come close. "Please, come and sit. Tell me what's going on with you."

"Frustration," Jim said as he followed Annie to the living room. "I need one more location to finish my book on abandoned places, and I'm not having much luck finding it." Jim and Alice took seats on the sofa. Boots immediately padded onto Alice's lap and curled up, giving Annie a smug look.

"Is her highness annoyed with you?" Alice asked as she rubbed the cat between the ears and was rewarded by a rumbling purr.

"I wouldn't let her sit in my lap earlier," Annie said. "She'll carry a grudge until dinnertime, and then all will be forgiven."

Jim leaned slightly away from Boots and shook his head. "Women and cats," he said. "I'll never really understand either."

Alice leaned over to give him a peck on the cheek. "It's the mystery that makes us interesting."

"And I do like a good mystery," Jim said.

Annie settled into the cozy chair across from the

sofa, smiling at her friends. Sometimes she worried about Alice's relationship with Jim. Annie knew Alice loved Stony Point and loved having roots here and a sense of community. She also knew Jim loved his nomadic life, moving from one job to the next with no roots anywhere. They seemed to have totally opposite goals, even though they both loved adventure. But Annie had to admit, Alice never looked happier than when Jim was around.

Jim ran a hand over his short silver beard. "I don't know where to look now," he said. "One place I had set up to shoot turned out to be a bust. It had a great story, but all the buildings were down to foundations. No visual interest. Another would have been a great shoot, but I couldn't get permission to get inside because the buildings were so decayed that the owner was scared I'd fall through a floor and sue him. Now my deadline is bearing down on me, and I need one last abandoned place with a juicy backstory."

"I wish I could help," Annie said. "The only abandoned place I know of around here is the Old Seaman's Rest, and it's not exactly photogenic."

"And I've seen more than enough of that place!" Alice said.

Annie knew that was true. Alice had spent the greater part of a day tied up in the Old Seaman's Rest building when she was kidnapped during a crazy mystery involving movie stars and swapped luggage.

"What kinds of spots do you have so far?" Annie asked.

"There's a ghost town out West," Jim said. "And an abandoned hospital, an abandoned prison, an abandoned amusement park, and a little village on an island in the middle of a river right here in Maine."

"I've seen some of the photos," Alice said. "They're enough to give you nightmares. You could set a really creepy movie in any of them."

"Then don't show them to me. Sometimes my imagination can be a little too vivid. I hope you find someplace," Annie said. "You don't have any leads at all?"

Jim shook his head. "I've chased a few, but they haven't turned into anything. I really need both a good story and good visuals. A ghost story would be best of all."

At that Annie laughed and picked up the book she'd left on the table. "You should read this then. It's one of my grandfather's books, and it has a witch, a curse, ghost dogs, and a family that abandoned their home."

"Really?" Jim's eyebrows rose in interest as he reached for the book.

"But I doubt the old family home is still there," Annie said. "Or if it is, it's probably not abandoned anymore. This is an old book."

Jim leafed through the book. "So, tell me the ghost story."

"Well, keep in mind that I haven't completely finished the book," Annie said. "It's the history of the Fuller family. Apparently it was written by a man my grandfather knew, or so it seems from the notes Grandpa scrawled in the page borders. The family owned an island off the coast of South Carolina."

"Oh!" Jim said. "Readers love Southern Gothic."

"Apparently the family was wealthy, fairly eccentric, and not well-liked by the mainlanders," Annie said. "Lots of stories went around about happenings on the island."

"What kind of happenings?"

Annie shrugged. "Apparently it depended on who you asked—everything from feuds to smuggling to practicing the dark arts."

"And which happening is the ghost story connected to?" Alice asked, her eyes shining.

"A little of all of them," Annie said. "From what I've read, the author's great-grandfather got into a feud with one of the mainland families over fishing near the island. Apparently the Fullers were very focused on privacy. Locals complained that they brought vicious guard dogs to the island for security to protect some sort of smuggling operation. Steven Fuller, the man who wrote this book, swore his family had not brought the dogs, and he hints that they actually were ghost dogs. At any rate, big black dogs were blamed for the attacks on several trespassers, and eventually, the author's great-grandfather was found mauled to death."

"By dogs?" Jim said.

"So the locals claim," Annie said. "The only other dangerous animals on the island were wild pigs."

"Pigs?" Alice said with a laugh.

Jim nodded. "Wild boar can be dangerous. I've run into a few in my time. One big fella got a little rowdy once ... so I ate him."

"You're such a tough guy," Alice told him.

"You know it," Jim said, his blue eyes sparkling. He turned back to Annie. "You said the family abandoned the island?"

"Apparently so," Annie said. "I don't yet know if they ever went back, but the great-grandfather's death was actually the last death blamed on the dogs. Apparently having a family member fall victim to the animals was too much, and the family abandoned the island. The author said the family believed the island was cursed, and that the empty land would always be guarded by these ghost dogs."

"Cursed?" Jim grinned. "It just gets better and better."

"That part is a little confusing," Annie said. "Actually, a lot of this book is a little confusing. But apparently an old woman from the family they feuded with placed a curse on them. The author's flowery style can make it a bit difficult to sort out all the particulars. Anyway, that's about as far as I got in the book, so I don't know what happens after that. I've been reading my grandfather's comments along with the text, and it makes it slow going."

"Charlie didn't take that sort of thing seriously, did he?" Alice said.

"Not the curses and such, of course," Annie answered. "But he did wonder about the dogs. He thought they might be a new breed. Apparently the scant description meant more to him than to me. Plus, if he knew the author, he might have heard about the dogs in more detail from him."

"Your grandfather was interested in dogs?" Jim asked.

Annie nodded. "He was a veterinarian."

Jim turned the book over in his hands. "Could I borrow this? I'd like to read it. It sounds like an intriguing possibility—*if* the island is still abandoned, and *if* there are any interesting ruins there."

"Feel free," Annie said, "as long as I get it back. I'm not done with it, but I have plenty of other books to fill my time while you use it."

"Don't worry," Jim said. "I wouldn't dare do anything to make Annie Dawson unhappy. You have a lot of fans in this town."

They chatted a bit longer after that, and Annie brought out iced tea and cookies, but she could tell by the way Jim kept sneaking peeks at the book that his mind was already off on his next assignment. She hoped she'd given him a good lead, though the more she thought of it, the less likely it seemed. Annie had lived in the Deep South, and the humidity was hard on buildings. An island abandoned since the turn of the century wasn't likely to be in good enough shape to offer many photographs for Jim's book.

She saw Jim settle back into the corner of the sofa and open the book again. At least she had cheered him up.

"Don't mind him," Alice said, giving Jim a look that he didn't even notice. "He's as bad as a treasure hunter sometimes."

"I just hope it turns out to be a treasure for his work," Annie said, "and not another disappointment."

"Well, if there's any photo treasures to be had," her friend said, "Jim will find them. You can count on it."

~ 2 ~

*I wasn't permitted to be in the room with the adults, of
course, and thus I sneaked in early to slip behind the old
camel-hair sofa. The dust and stiff hair made me want to
sneeze. I was a child, barely six years old. I remember the air
in the room was thick, almost stifling, with smoke from cigars
and pipes. The men in the room were all my family and my
heroes. I knew in my young heart that these men could face
down lions, but their voices quaked as they whispered about
the dogs. I heard about the red eyes, the jaws dripping with
blood, and the horrible sound of their howls that cut the night
air with dire prediction like the scream of a banshee.*

—Steven Fuller, 1925

Since she'd sent the book with Jim, Annie spent the rest
of the weekend on normal autumn chores. She raked
up the rest of her leaves and dumped them into her leaf
compost bins. Since not all the leaves were off the trees, she
knew that no matter how clear she managed to get the lawn,
the next good wind would mean more raking.

On Monday, she headed into town and bought two big
maroon mums for her front porch. As she set them out, she
smiled, remembering the year she'd bought so many mums
from a local school fundraiser that she couldn't even get on
the porch. Thankfully Ian had saved her from herself and

found someone to come and take most of the flowers off her hands.

Annie was a little surprised not to see Alice or Jim again. She wondered if Jim had made any headway on finding the location he needed for his book. Annie was fairly sure that not even a visit from the handsome photographer would keep Alice from a Hook and Needle Club meeting, so she was glad when Tuesday arrived, and she could head into town to catch up with everyone.

When the bell tinkled to signal her arrival at A Stitch in Time, Annie felt a warm rush as Mary Beth Brock looked up from her spot at the register and smiled. "You're early today!"

"I see I still didn't beat Stella," Annie answered, smiling and nodding toward the elderly woman in the smart blue suit. Stella Brickson nodded back with the silent dignity of a queen bestowing favor. Then she bent her white-haired head back over her knitting.

"*I* barely beat Stella here on Tuesdays," Mary Beth answered.

Annie looked around the bright, cozy shop. "Where's Kate?"

Kate Stevens was Mary Beth Brock's assistant and one of the most talented crochet designers Annie had ever seen. She'd even won a prestigious design competition with one of her lovely dresses.

"She came in this morning looking like a ghost, and I sent her home," Mary Beth said. "Apparently she ate some questionable seafood over the weekend and spent all day yesterday ill."

Annie winced. "Poor thing. Does she need someone to pick up Vanessa from school or get her anything?"

"No, I checked," Mary Beth said.

Annie nodded. Mary Beth could be a bit of a mother hen, so Annie was sure she had things well in hand. As Annie turned toward the circle of overstuffed chairs to join Stella, she heard the tinkle of the bell behind her.

Gwendolyn Palmer and Peggy Carson walked in together. They were an interesting study in contrasts. Peggy had the exuberance of youth, was full-figured, and had shiny black hair. Gwen wore her pale blond hair short and was the perfect image of a handsome woman of means. Peggy's pink uniform from The Cup & Saucer was slightly rumpled from a busy morning shift, while Gwen's soft wool suit and matching silver sweater hung on her thin frame perfectly. Their sparkling eyes and bright smiles were definitely something they shared as they greeted everyone; there was no class warfare when it came to the Hook and Needle Club.

Mary Beth explained again about Kate as everyone took a seat. Annie kept glancing toward the door, hoping to see Alice. She tried to tell herself firmly that her curious nature was constantly getting her in trouble, and that she should rein it in—but then her eyes would dart to the door again.

"What's keeping Alice?" Gwen asked, noticing Annie's distraction.

"I'm not sure," Annie said.

Peggy giggled. "I have an idea. I saw her and Jim Parker in the diner for breakfast. He always reminds me of a pirate.

Maybe he's whisked her away for an adventure."

Stella looked up from her knitting with a sniff. "He looks untidy with that scruffy beard."

"Pirates generally *do* look untidy," Gwen said. "It's part of the appeal."

"I'm surprised you like that sort of thing," Stella responded. "Your John always looks so neat."

"Not always," Gwen said with a small smile. Then she turned her attention very intently to her own knitting to discourage possible questions on *that* subject.

"What about you, Annie?" Peggy asked, her voice teasing. "Do you like the pirate type or someone who's tidy?"

"I just like that Jim makes Alice happy," Annie said. She hoped to divert a storm of Ian-related teasing since she suspected it was on the horizon.

"He does seem to do that," Stella grudgingly agreed.

At that, the bell over the door tinkled again and every eye turned as Alice rushed into the shop. "Sorry I'm late," she said. "I was tied up."

"See?" Peggy whispered loudly. "Pirate! Arr!"

All the women laughed. Alice put her hands on her hips and looked at the group with a mock frown. "Did I miss something?"

"Peggy was telling us that Jim Parker is in town," Mary Beth said.

Alice nodded and took a seat with the rest of the club. "He may not be much longer. He's trying to track down a family from South Carolina so he can get permission to shoot photos on their island."

"Oh?" Annie said. "So he read the book?"

"What book?" Peggy asked.

Annie explained about the book she'd found in the attic of Grey Gables and Jim's interest in it. "I do hope it'll prove to be a good lead for him."

"I'm glad to hear you say that," Alice said. "I'm on computer search duty, and I was hoping we could do it together. Between the two of us, we make about one experienced Web surfer."

"I don't mind trying," Annie said.

"A trip to South Carolina would be wonderful," Mary Beth said. "It would certainly be much cooler to go south this time of year than when we made the road trip for the needlework convention in Texas."

"I've been to Charleston in the fall," Annie said. "It's lovely. I don't know how far away the island is from there though."

"I don't know either, but I might find out firsthand," Alice said, blushing slightly. "Jim asked me to go along if this lead pans out."

"Oh?" Mary Beth said, her voice rising. "What happened to your being so busy with Divine Décor parties that you couldn't make it to the needlework convention with us? Hmm?"

Alice grew a bit pinker, but she just laughed at the teasing. "Things tend to slow down a little in September and October, then go crazy with the Christmas buying rush in November. I think I can squeeze in a little trip."

"Right," Peggy said. "It has nothing to do with getting to spend time with a handsome pirate."

Alice laughed. "Pirate? Hardly. He gets seasick."

Peggy shrugged. "OK. If not a pirate, maybe an adventurer like Indiana Jones."

"That I can agree with," Alice said. Then she clapped her hands. "So can we move on from talking about my love life? Any big projects for the club?"

"Well, since you mentioned it," Mary Beth said, "the little needlework group at the Seaside Hills Assisted Living facility asked me about taking part in a gift drive for the families who lost homes during the tornado season last spring. They want to do slippers, warm hats, scarves, afghans—things like that. I promised I would ask everyone."

"What would be the target date for sending the things in?" Stella asked.

"Mid-November," Mary Beth said.

"That sounds like a good idea," Annie said. "I can't imagine losing everything to something so unpredictable and uncontrollable."

"I'm in," Peggy said. "I have a cute pattern for quilted boot slippers. I was going to make a pair for Emily for Christmas."

"Let me guess," Alice said. "Purple ones, right?"

Peggy laughed. "Is there any other color?"

"I'm in too," Gwen said. "I could do several warm hats by that deadline."

"And I'll be happy to join in," Stella added. "I would like to do mittens."

"I'll try a scarf," Alice said. "It'll let me practice my fairly weak attempts at crochet."

"Then we're all agreed?" Mary Beth said. At the nods,

she added. "I'll call Joan McTavish, and she can pass the word to the other ladies."

The women continued to chat about needlework for a while longer before Peggy yelped and announced she had to run back to the diner. "Time always flies at our meetings!" she moaned as she gathered up her things.

As always, that was the signal for everyone to begin putting away supplies and stuffing projects back into bags. Annie saw Gwen carry a piece of knitting over to Stella, and the two women peered at the stitches together. Both women were master knitters, and Annie always enjoyed seeing their intricate work.

Annie folded her own half-done afghan carefully and slipped it back in the bag. She thought she'd contribute it to the tornado victims once it was done and maybe crochet a few hats to go with it. Simple ribbed winter hats were quick to make.

"Do you want to join me for lunch at The Cup & Saucer and then hit the computer?" Alice asked.

Annie turned and smiled. "I heard you'd already been to the diner once today."

Alice nodded. "True, and so normally I would suggest Maplehurst Inn, but since the diner is so close to the library … ."

"Peggy will tease you," Annie warned.

"I'll be brave."

They said their goodbyes to the others and headed out. Annie shivered at the slight chill in the breeze and pulled her cardigan closer around her. "The sunshine fooled me this morning," she said. "I wish now that I'd worn a jacket."

"That's one thing driving a convertible does for me," Alice said. "I always dress a little more warmly because I know I'm going to feel some wind."

"It also means you have the most extensive collection of scarves of anyone I know," Annie said.

"That's me, the fashionista," Alice said with a laugh.

Thankfully, the walk to the diner was short, and soon the slightly moist warmth of the diner engulfed Annie. She sighed with the combined pleasure of the warmth and the delicious aroma coming from the kitchen.

"Wow, you *do* love our food," Peggy said to Alice as she met them at the door. "Are you two joining Jim?"

"Jim's still here?" Alice said in surprise.

Peggy nodded across the room where Jim sat at a corner booth with a cellphone to his ear. "I think the diner is his new office."

"He looks busy," Annie said.

"We'll have our own table," Alice agreed, and then she smiled mischievously. "Just make it a table near his."

"You got it," Peggy said, leading them across the room. "Do you need menus? The corn chowder is yummy today."

"I'll just have that," Annie said. "With coffee."

"Same for me."

They sat down without Jim even glancing in their direction.

"I didn't even ask. Are you OK with doing the research at the library? I could bring my laptop over to your house, and we could work at the table in the kitchen if you'd rather," Alice said. "The computers are faster at the library, however, and Jim says he needs to do a little cleanup on my laptop."

"You have a virus?" Annie asked in alarm.

Alice shrugged. "I'm not sure. It isn't threatening me with doom or shutting down. Honestly, I know how to make the computer do what I need, but I'm not all that technologically savvy. I just know Jim was tsk-tsking over it."

Annie nodded. "Herb made those kinds of noises over mine when they were here." Actually her daughter LeeAnn's husband had just sat and shook his head as he fixed a problem she was having with her email. Annie had the sinking feeling that her grandchildren were going to be a lot more technologically gifted than she was.

Alice snuck a glance over at Jim at almost the same moment he ended his call and looked up. The smile that spread over his face was like watching the sun rise.

"Ah, the two most beautiful ladies in Stony Point," he said. "Are you two going to join me?"

"We didn't want to intrude on your work," Annie said.

"You're not intruding," Jim said as the women got up and joined him in the booth. He scooted over to allow Alice to sit beside him, while Annie took the seat on the other side of the table. "You're cheering me up. I still haven't tracked down any of the Fuller family, but I did call the historical society in the closest mainland town—Preacher's Reach. They had a little information on the Fullers."

"Well, that's good," Alice said. "Anything juicy?"

"Apparently Steven Fuller, the man who wrote the family history, returned to the island not long after that book was published. He was some kind of doctor and opened a private hospital on the island."

"That sounds interesting," Annie said.

"Especially since no one knew what kind of hospital," Jim said. "Apparently the general gossip was that it was a lunatic asylum for the wealthy."

"And what happened to it?" Alice asked.

"The woman at the historical society had a newspaper clip. The hospital closed when Steven Fuller disappeared after one of the patients was killed in a wild animal attack on the island."

"The dogs again?" Annie asked.

Jim took a sip of his coffee. "The clipping didn't say. But the woman did have one more interesting clipping. Steven Fuller had one child, a daughter, and the clipping was of her wedding to a man named Maynard Cole. So, we might need to track the family through that line."

Annie pulled a notebook out of her project bag and wrote down the name. Then she slipped the notebook into her cardigan pocket as Peggy arrived with the soup. The smooth, creamy soup was full of soft potatoes, corn, and bacon. Annie's attention was totally caught up in the haze of the delicious soup for a while.

"So now, you might be taking pictures of a spooky house that was *also* an asylum," Alice said after sipping her soup. "Did the historical society have anything else on the ghost stories of the island?"

"She emphatically told me there was no ghost activity on the island. She used those words, 'ghost activity.'" Jim shook his head. "You never know what you're going to run into with historical societies. Sometimes they love to tell stories and gossip. Sometimes they're completely closed-mouthed about anything they can't document

and fiercely protective about the reputation of local people. I suspect the society at Preacher's Reach is more the
latter kind."

"Hopefully, we'll have better luck with the Internet,"
Alice said. "What will you do while we're surfing the Web?"

"I need to talk to my publisher," he said. "Even if this
island is perfect, and we get permission, I'm still going to
have to push back my deadline a little." He sighed. "This
will be the first deadline I've ever missed. On the other
hand, since it's the first extension I've ever needed, my publisher should agree to it."

"They'll be thrilled when they get the finished product,"
Alice said. "Especially if you wrap it up with a really spooky
location."

Suddenly Annie felt an icy chill. She shivered and pulled
her sweater closer, looking around for where the draft might
have come from. Not seeing anything, she turned her attention back to her soup, shaking off the nagging fear that it
was some kind of premonition. She didn't believe in witches,
ghost dogs, and that sort of thing, but some of her thoughts
of foreboding had been right several times in the past.

Still, she was sure there was nothing to worry about.

~ 3 ~

*In front of strangers, every member of my family said the
same thing: wild boar. No one wanted to be connected with a
mad story of curses and demon hounds. As a boy, I was a true
believer in the hounds. The death of my great-grandfather
had come at the time of my greatest weakness—a time when
imagination was far more interesting than reality. I'm no longer a little boy, but a man and a scientist. I no longer peek
under my bed or worry about the partially open door to my
closet. Though, if honest, I would admit that the lonely howl
of a hound in the night still makes me shiver.*

—Steven Fuller, 1925

After lunch, Annie and Alice headed to the library. The
beautiful Greek Revival–style building never failed
to impress Annie. The library she always used back
in Brookfield, Texas, was sprawling, squat, and modern.
Annie liked the feeling of history the Stony Point Public
Library projected, with its bright white siding, black
shutters, and columns.

Main Street in Stony Point was rarely noisy, but it was
almost hushed as Alice and Annie stepped through the mul-
tipaned glass door leading to the library foyer. The softening
of sound always made Annie feel like she was stepping into
a different world.

That sense of otherworldliness was broken as soon as they approached the circulation desk. Valerie Duffy, wearing a fall jacket decorated with pumpkins and black cats, greeted them with a smile. "Whenever I see you two together, I wonder what kind of mystery is afoot," she said.

"This is less mystery and more research project," Alice said. "Annie and I are going to play dueling computers."

"You picked a good time," Valerie said, coming around the desk to lead them toward the computer area. "After school lets out, the computers tend to be very busy."

"Then we'll have to hurry," Annie said, glancing down at her watch.

Valerie held out the clipboard with the sign-up sheets. "Since it's quiet, you can go ahead and sign up for two hours, if you want. We still have one more open computer if anyone comes in."

Annie sat in the worn wooden chair in front of the computer station. She scooted the mouse, and the screen in front of her snapped quickly from the screensaver to the search engine. She slipped the notebook out of her pocket and typed in "Steven Fuller" and "Preacher's Reach."

The combination produced two links, and both were a bit eccentric. The first connected to a Web page on a site for paranormal researchers in South Carolina. The other connected to a site about "Adventuring" in the South. Annie clicked on that link first and quickly learned "adventuring" was apparently a euphemism for trespassing on private property.

The text below the video window said two anonymous adventurers had rowed out to Fuller's Island at night to make a film for their website. Annie clicked on the video link. At first, she thought there must be something wrong since the little box remained dark. Then she realized it was simply the result of filming at night.

She picked up the headphones that were next to the computer and put them on. She could hear a young woman's breathless whispering along with the sound of a boat scraping across the sand. "I'm sure the canoe is out of sight here," the young woman said. "We don't dare turn on flashlights until we're out of sight of shore."

"Come on," a male voice urged.

The screen was still dark. Annie heard brush crashing and the sound of breathing. She shook her head, amused, as the black screen remained, and she just heard more breathing and crashing. Finally she heard a larger crash and muffled swearing from the man. "That's it!" he said. "Turn on the light!"

A light flashed on, illuminating the face of a thin young man in his mid-twenties sprawled on the ground. He quickly swung up his arm in front of his face. "Not in my eyes," he grumbled. "Now I really can't see."

"Sorry," the woman said.

The light swung quickly away from the young man, and Annie could see overgrown brush faintly lit by the flashlight. "Which way to the house?" the woman asked, swinging the camera back toward the man.

He pointed ahead. "The path leads to the buildings. Just keep the light out of my face." Then he turned and began pushing through the overgrowth. The camera mostly filmed the back of his head for a while.

Annie felt Alice lean over close to her. "What are you watching?"

"Adventurers on Fuller's Island," Annie said. "They mostly seem to be stumbling around in the dark."

Alice chuckled as she watched the screen. Mostly it revealed barely lit foliage and the back of the young man's head. "Not exactly an award-winning documentary," she said.

Annie nodded, slipping the earphones from her head to share with Alice. Suddenly the two people in the video stumbled into a clearing, and the beam of the flashlight carried a bit farther into the darkness. The corner of a darkly stained cinder-block wall reflected back at them in the beam. A thick vine with broad leaves climbed up the wall, hiding much of it from view.

The camera swung back to the man as he turned and asked, "Do you hear that?"

"I heard something." The woman's voice sounded a little shaky.

"I think it was a dog!"

The woman sounded doubtful. "I didn't hear it clearly enough to be sure."

The audio had more sounds of moving through brush, as well as some wet squishy noises that suggested the ground was mostly mud. The cinder-block building grew closer, and Annie could see a deep crack running through several of the blocks. She hoped the couple didn't plan to go into the building. It didn't look safe.

Then a distinct howl sounded from the distance. "*That* was a dog," the man insisted.

"I don't think it's close," the woman said.

"But it's on the island. We have confirmation of at least one dog on—" his voice dropped as another howl sounded, clearer and closer. "Either that dog moves awfully fast, or there's more than one. Maybe we should head back."

"We haven't seen anything," she said.

The sound of muffled barking and more howls rang out, and the man simply pushed past the woman and ran. A snarl sounded close—very close. The woman spun, camera pointing at her feet as she ran. She slammed into something, the picture jerking on the camera. Then it fell to the ground. All it showed was foliage, but the sound of snuffling proved the dogs had caught up. Annie heard another snarl and the snap of teeth. Then the video ended.

"Well, that got a lot more exciting at the end," she said.

Alice leaned close to her screen. "Let me copy down that URL. Jim is going to want to see that."

"He's welcome to it," Annie said. "I know I don't care to see it again. Those dogs sounded big."

Alice nodded. "I wonder if the island has security. Those could have been guard dogs."

"That only makes them scarier."

Alice chuckled at that and turned back to her computer. Annie navigated back to the paranormal investigation site. Thankfully, it didn't have any videos. There was only a brief mention of the group's desire to do an "investigation" on Fuller's Island. The site mentioned that the owner of the island lived in Boston, but it didn't list a name. "Alice, look at this!"

Alice leaned over, her eyes sweeping over the text. "That's great. At least we know where to look, even if we don't know who we're looking for. I'm trying some genealogy sites."

Annie turned to watch as Alice went through searches on several sites. She entered both "Steven Fuller" and "Maynard Cole."

Annie turned back to her computer and tried a general search engine. She typed in the names from the list and then added "genealogy" before clicking on the search link. The search engine reported no results for that combination so she changed "genealogy" to "family tree." This time she found a link to a school project posted online by Becky Cole. The child had traced her family tree back through Maynard Cole and Steven Fuller, and even further to other Fullers. "That's it!"

Alice turned back to Annie's computer again and grinned. "That's it all right. Let me print that."

As she sent the command to the library printer, Valerie Duffy leaned over to whisper, "We have some kids who need the computers for homework."

Annie glanced at the time read-out on the computer. She'd had no idea so much time had passed while they clicked around, read, and watched the video.

"We're done," Alice said. "I just need to pay for the things I printed."

Valerie smiled. "Great. I'll tell the kids they can have your spots."

Annie followed Alice to the printer where she gathered the small pile of papers. "Now all Jim has to do is find an address for ...," she paused and looked at the last page of the printout, "Robert Cole."

"And hope he gives permission," Annie added.

"Jim can be very persuasive," Alice said.

Annie grinned at her friend. "You would know."

I don't believe my great-grandmother ever completely recovered from the death of her husband. She settled in with my uncle and aunt at their plantation home in Charleston. Though well away from Fuller's Island, they weren't completely away from the scandal. No one in society made remarks to my great-grandmother's face, of course, but she withdrew from everyone. I saw her ghostly thin figure only a few times, and in my memories, she always seemed a bit like Miss Havisham in Great Expectations.

—Steven Fuller, 1925

*I*t didn't take Jim Parker long to track down a phone number to go with the name Annie had found. When it came time to make the call, Jim invited Annie and Alice to listen in. "I wouldn't have gotten this far, this fast, without you two," he said.

They had gathered in Alice's bright and airy living room. Annie had to smile at how much Jim looked out of place next to Alice's light, feminine furniture and decor. She was reminded of Peggy's remark about Jim looking like a pirate. Right now, he seemed like a pirate having tea with the queen.

"What are you smiling about?" Alice asked.

"Just woolgathering," Annie said. Then she turned

to Jim. "Did you watch the website video that was made on the island?"

Jim nodded with a wry smile. "Looked like gullible kids scaring each other in the dark to me."

"But you have to admit," Alice said. "there were definitely dogs."

"I'll ask the owner if he uses dogs in the security there," Jim said, taking a deep breath as he fished out his phone. "Assuming he'll talk to me, that is."

"Just charm him," Alice said.

"I'm not that charming."

"You charmed me."

Jim's slow smile showed off a slightly crooked front tooth. "You're a special case."

Annie cleared her throat. "You need to call, or I have to go home. I embarrass easily."

Jim and Alice laughed, and then he punched the numbers into his phone. He introduced himself to Robert Cole, explained that he had Alice and Annie in the room and asked if he could switch to speakerphone. After getting Mr. Cole's permission, Jim explained his interest in Fuller's Island. "I believe the island would make an excellent addition to my book, Mr. Cole." he said finally.

"I haven't been on the island in years," the man said. "Most of the buildings probably aren't safe."

"I'll be glad to sign a waiver," Jim assured him, "holding you totally blameless if I'm fool enough to fall through a floor somewhere."

Jim coaxed the man for a few more minutes, and finally Mr. Cole gave a hesitant agreement. "But I want to have that waiver in my possession before you step one foot on the island."

"I'll fax you a copy and then drop the original in the mail," Jim said. "How's that?"

"OK," the man said. "I'd tell you not to damage anything, but I expect there's not much left to damage."

"Don't forget to call your security," Alice said. "So they know we're coming."

"Security?" Mr. Cole said. "I don't have anyone on the island, lady. Like I said, there's nothing really there to damage, and I've got the land posted for no trespassing. Beyond that, I'm not throwing good money at it."

"So you don't have anyone on the island with dogs?" Alice asked.

"Oh please!" The man's voice grew sharper. "I hope you're not planning to dredge up too much of that ghost-dog garbage. I spend enough time fielding ghost-hunter calls. I don't need someone getting a fresh surge going."

"No, I'm interested in the images of how the island has changed through time," Jim said soothingly. "And anything I run with will be about the history of the island."

"All right," Mr. Cole said. "Then I agree, but don't forget that waiver."

"I won't," Jim promised. They talked a bit longer about the best place to land a boat on the island, and then Jim hung up.

"Wow, no security," Alice said. "So where did the dogs come from?"

Jim's grin turned wicked. "I guess we'll have to head down and find out. You're coming with me aren't you, Red?"

Alice smiled. "To a haunted island with killer ghost dogs? You do know how to show a girl a good time."

Jim laughed. "Always."

"Are you sure about all of this, Alice?" Annie asked, shaking her head at her friends. She was glad it was Alice heading off to the island and not her. She didn't believe in ghosts, of course, but it didn't sound like ghosts on the video. And she wasn't in any big hurry to get bitten by wild dogs. "I hope you'll both be careful."

"Don't worry," Jim said. "I'll take good care of my girl."

Annie smiled. "Take good care of each other, and I'll be happy."

"I promise to send constant updates," Alice said. "You just watch your email. I'll send mission reports. Maybe I should do videos like those kids."

"Just don't make any in the dark," Annie replied. "You'll only give me nightmares."

Jim pulled his laptop out of a bag on the floor and opened it on his lap. "I actually found some satellite images of the island online," he said, as the computer booted up. "You can tell there are still buildings there, so I'm hoping for some good shots."

As soon as the computer booted up, Jim clicked over to the site with the satellite photographs and typed in the location. At first, the picture was of the whole southeast coast, but as he clicked closer and closer, it began to focus on the island.

Finally, they could see the tops of buildings showing between dense clumps of trees. He clicked closer still, and they could see huge gaps in the roof of one of the buildings.

"That one is looking a little rough," Alice said.

Jim nodded. "The floors are probably going to be bad in there. We might not be able to go in, but it would be great to shoot up from inside and show the sky."

Alice pointed to a smaller building, more obscured by the treetop canopy. "That one looks solid though," she said.

Jim nodded. "We won't know for sure until we get there, but I think these will be enough to appease my publisher. It looks like a great spot."

The next few days, Annie didn't see much of her friends as they prepared for their trip south. They did come to Grey Gables one afternoon for a particularly confusing session involving setting up Annie's laptop with a program for video chats so she could keep in touch with Alice.

"This way I can see if the ghost dogs manage to make your hair turn white with fright," Annie said when she'd finally figured out how the program worked. "Just no scary live movies from the island."

"No worries," Jim said. "I doubt the ghosts have Wi-Fi, we won't be able to send email or video-chat each day until we're back on the mainland."

"In a nice hotel," Alice said. "Or maybe a bed and breakfast. I bet there are some gorgeous B&Bs in South Carolina."

"You know, that might be an idea for my next project," Jim said. "Haunted B&Bs. Those old ones have as many ghost stories as lighthouses."

"I think I saw one of those on television," Alice said. "The Myrtles Plantation in Louisiana. I thought it would be fun to stay there."

"You have a strange definition of fun," Annie said with a shiver.

Alice's eyes sparkled with excitement. "Don't you think it would be a fantastic adventure?"

Annie smiled at her friend. Alice had been wild about adventure since they were kids. Annie would visit her grandparents in Maine during the summer while her parents were on mission trips out of the country. It was those summertime visits that had sealed a friendship that had revived when Annie returned to Stony Point and Grey Gables after the death of her grandmother. Back in the day, Alice often dragged Annie into things that she would never try on her own.

"I actually like tamer entertainment," Annie said, "like walking on the beach and picking up shells."

"Chicken," Alice teased.

"You can't get me to take dares now. I can totally live with being a chicken in my old age."

"Old age?" Jim pointed at her. "You don't fool anyone, Annie Dawson. I've seen you take on some big scary things when you felt it was important."

"But not ghost dogs," Annie said. "You can call me when you come across ghost bunnies or ghost kittens, something small."

"Ghost mice!" Alice suggested, and then she giggled when Annie shivered. She'd had more than enough trouble with *real* mice at Grey Gables in the past.

"I will want to hear all about your adventure though," Annie added. "But if you do anything dangerous, don't tell me about it until you get home. Otherwise, I'll worry."

"You'll worry anyway," Alice said.

"A little." Annie stood up and closed her laptop. "Can I get you two some more coffee?"

"None for me," Jim said. "My doctor says I need to stop living on coffee and stubbornness. We should head on to dinner. I have reservations at Maplehurst Inn. Do you want to join us?"

Annie shook her head. "Three's a crowd."

"You're always welcome with us," Jim said. "Especially since I'm whisking Red away for at least a couple of weeks."

"Yes, Annie, come on along for dinner."

Annie smiled but shook her head again. "You've convinced me that I'm welcome, but I think I'll still have to pass. I want to call LeeAnn and talk to the twins. LeeAnn is considering buying the twins a pet as soon as they can both agree on one. I want to see if they've reached a meeting of the minds yet."

"Grandkids," Jim said. "I guess that's something I missed out on, never settling down."

"Well, you have to make it through having kids first," Alice said. "And they grow up to be teenagers. Every time I get all mushy over kids, I just remember what I put my mom through in *my* teen years. It snaps me right out of it."

"LeeAnn worried Wayne and me half to death a time or two," Annie admitted, "but it was worth it."

"I'll take your word for it," Jim said as he held out a crooked elbow for Alice. "Shall we go, milady?"

"Anywhere you want."

After Annie closed the door behind her friends, she felt a small whisper of wistfulness. It would be nice to have romance in her life again. Since her husband, Wayne, died,

Annie was often flooded with the little thoughtful and romantic things he did so often. Wayne never wanted them to become just old married people. He wanted to keep the romantic spark, and he'd worked hard at it. Annie felt now like she might have taken that almost for granted. She sure missed it now. She missed Wayne.

With a sad sigh, she turned from the door and headed for the comfy sofa. Time to call LeeAnn and be reminded of the things that remained in her life.

*   *   *   *

After Alice and Jim left on their trip, Alice was as good as her word. Every night she either logged in for a video chat or sent an email about her day. Annie found she loved experiencing the adventure from a nice, safe distance, especially since Alice always made her experiences so vivid when she talked.

"So, are the local people getting used to you?" Annie asked on the third night. "Have they gotten any friendlier?"

"Not a scrap," Alice said. "They still act like they think we're carpet-bagging Yankees."

Annie shook her head. "I don't think they're likely to be hanging on to Civil War resentment; maybe they're just shy about strangers."

"They're hanging on to *something*," Alice said. "I tell you, if Jim hadn't flashed some serious cash, we'd have never gotten our rooms at this inn. I don't know the last time I've gotten this many dirty looks."

"I hope the island has been interesting," Annie said.

"It's fantastic," Alice said. "I don't know what dogs those kids ran into, but we haven't seen anything like that. It's just creepy old buildings and twisted trees dripping with moss. I can see why we had to sign waivers though. Some of the buildings are held up by memories and kudzu."

"I'm looking forward to seeing the photos. It sounds fascinating."

"We found some mysterious medical equipment in one of the buildings," Alice said. "Jim got some very creepy photos of it."

"Are the buildings safe to go into?" Annie asked. "On the satellite images, they looked pretty run-down."

"Some are a little shaky for me, but Jim is fearless," Alice said. "Speaking of fearless, we're going to do some early-evening shoots because Jim was hoping to catch some nocturnal wildlife in some shots."

Annie smiled. "Oh? Will a possum or raccoon add to the ambiance?"

"I never question the artiste," Alice said, "but I might miss a check-in with you one night. I'll email though."

Annie kept Alice's promise in mind the next night when she didn't show up for their video chat. "I hope Jim found a photogenic possum," Annie said as she scooped up Boots and carried her off to the bedroom. Boots blinked at her and offered a sleepy meow.

*   *   *   *

Two days passed with no word from Alice. Eventually, Annie kept her laptop set up all the time on the kitchen table, plugged into the wall to save the battery. She didn't want to miss getting an email from Alice.

On Tuesday morning, Annie was gathering her crochet project to take with her to the Hook and Needle Club, but she squeezed in one last email check. She felt her stomach clench just a bit tighter when she still had no messages.

Annie knew she could be a bit of a worrier, but Alice had promised to email, but she hadn't. And her cellphone was sending Annie's calls straight to voice mail. Since Annie didn't know the name of the inn where Alice was staying, she couldn't just call there. With each passing hour, the feeling increased that something was very wrong. Alice was too considerate to leave Annie worried—not if she could help it.

As she headed out the door, she decided to squeeze in a quick stop by Ian's office before heading to A Stitch in Time. Ian could be counted on for calm, clear advice, and Annie felt the need for a little reassurance.

As she pulled into a parking space in front of A Stitch in Time, Annie smiled at the sight of the Lincoln Continental in the next space. Stella was probably already seated in one of the cozy chairs inside, her needles clicking at full speed. Annie looked between the needlework shop and Town Hall—if she went to see Ian, she was sure to be late for the meeting.

Finally, she headed across the street. She didn't want to talk to everyone at the Hook and Needle Club while she was so worried. Once Ian helped her find some perspective, she would be able to tell her friends about Alice without any hysteria.

Annie crossed Town Square quickly and trotted up the steps to the imposing Town Hall. She'd been inside many times, of course. The happy visits were always to see Ian, but she'd made more than a few stops at the Stony Point Police Department as well. Annie's tendency to attract mysteries had put her in danger more than once, and she had good reason to appreciate the police force.

As she strode across the airy foyer, her eyes were drawn to the glass case with its display of work by local artisans. The beautiful colors and patterns in the display never failed to make her smile. Stony Point was home to so many talented people.

She turned down the hallway toward Ian's office. As always, she was halted in her tracks by the imposing stare of Ian's secretary, Charlotte Nash. Annie happened to know Charlotte had a lovely smile when she used it, but she guarded the mayor's time with all the seriousness of a palace guard.

"Hi Charlotte," Annie said. "Do you know if Ian has a minute?"

"I'll ask." Charlotte looked purposefully toward a bench a few feet away. Considering how avidly she listened to every scrap of gossip that passed through Town Hall, Charlotte was very careful about keeping her own conversations private.

Annie obediently walked to the bench and sat, knowing that everything went smoother when Charlotte got her way. She had barely sat down when Ian's office door opened, and he walked out with a huge smile. "Annie," he said. "What a pleasure!"

Annie was surprised at the sense of relief that washed over her. It was as if a tiny part of her now relaxed; she counted on Ian to take care of the problem. Annie frowned slightly at the thought. She liked to think of herself as more independent than that.

Ian stopped at her frown. "Oh no, don't tell me I'm in trouble."

Annie smiled. "No, not at all. I do have something I'd like to talk to you about."

"Shall we go into my office?" Ian asked.

Annie nodded and followed him quietly.

When Annie walked into the office, Ian gestured to one of the handsome leather chairs that faced his desk. As she sat, he took the other chair so they wouldn't have the desk between them. "So what's wrong?" he asked, half-jokingly. "More trouble from your attic?"

Annie smiled slightly. Ian knew how often things from the attic in Grey Gables came with a mystery attached to them. "No, this time my problem is more human," she said. "I'm worried about Alice."

Ian looked surprise. "I thought she went on some photo shoot with Jim Parker."

"She did," Annie said. "They went to South Carolina to take photographs on an island I told them about. But Alice was contacting me every night to recap the day's work, and I haven't heard from her in over two days."

"Two days doesn't seem terribly long," Ian said reassuringly. "Maybe they're just busy."

"I'm sure they are busy," Annie agreed, "but Alice and I were connecting every night through a video chat that Jim set up for us. And she promised that if she couldn't get on to chat, she would email. But I've heard nothing for two days, and all my calls to her are going to voice mail."

Ian frowned, deep in thought. "Well, Jim Parker has taken far too many chances with Alice—and with you—in the past. Still, I know he cares about Alice. I don't think he would let anything happen to her."

Annie nodded. "But they're exactly alike when it comes to chasing adventure, and I'm worried that it's gotten them into trouble."

"You know," Ian said, sitting back in the chair, "their trip could have turned—how should I word this?—*romantic*. That could certainly make them forget about other people for a while."

"I hadn't considered that." Annie ran a hand through her straight blond hair. "I suppose that could have happened. Still, Alice knows I would worry."

Ian's face darkened again. "She certainly knows that, and Alice wouldn't want to be the cause of that kind of concern. Do you happen to know where they're staying?"

Annie shook her head. "I know the closest mainland town is Preacher's Reach, and Alice said they were staying in an inn. But I don't know its name."

"Why don't you let me look into what inns are in the area," Ian said. "Then I could ask Chief Edwards to make some calls. He'd get a straight answer quicker than I could. We can at least find out where they're staying."

Again, Annie felt a wash of relief. "Thank you, Ian. I knew you would help me."

"I'm just happy you thought of me," Ian said, smiling.

"You know, we're likely to find that they just got so caught up in their adventure that they forgot. You very well could get a sheepish call from Alice by tonight."

"I hope so," Annie said fervently. "I truly hope so."

— 5 —

My great-grandfather's home always felt oppressively dark to me as a young child. It had plenty of windows—tall windows that were frequently cast open to catch any hope of breeze in the summer—but the island was so full of trees that the light all over the island felt weak as if it were sickly. My mother fretted about disease on the island. I was more concerned about monsters.

—*Steven Fuller, 1925*

Feeling considerably better, Annie hurried back across Town Square, hoping she hadn't missed all of the Hook and Needle Club meeting. She was happy to see the white Lincoln still parked in front of the shop.

Everyone looked up to smile at her as she hurried into the shop.

"I was afraid you were going to stand us up," Mary Beth said.

"Especially when Peggy saw you dashing toward the mayor's office," Gwen added.

"And that's why there is no point trying to keep a secret in Stony Point," Kate said with a laugh. Kate had experienced plenty of teasing over the handsome police detective she'd met in Texas at the needlework convention they'd attended, and Annie doubted there was anyone in Stony Point who *didn't* know all the details. Of course, distance had dampened that relationship fairly quickly.

"Welcome back, Kate," Annie said as she walked over to take an empty chair beside Gwen. "Glad to see you're feeling better."

Annie then addressed the rest of the group. "I wanted to ask Ian's opinion about something," she said. "Now I would like to ask yours."

"You know how we *love* to give our opinions," Mary Beth said.

Peggy giggled. "That's for sure!"

Annie explained about Alice's promise to keep in touch and how they'd used video chat. "But I haven't heard a word for two days," she said. "And when I've called, her phone goes straight to voice mail."

Peggy grinned. "Maybe she's busy with her pirate."

"Maybe," Annie said doubtfully.

The gentle clicking of Stella's knitting needles stopped and the older woman set her knitting down carefully in her lap before turning intense eyes toward Annie. "Nonsense," she said. "Alice takes her word seriously. After being married to that rat John MacFarlane, she certainly knows how painful it is when you can't count on someone's word. If she said she would contact Annie, she would do it—unless she *can't*."

Annie felt the sting of tears as Stella gave voice to exactly what was worrying her. "That's what I thought," she said. "Alice knows how much this would worry me."

The women's faces all grew very serious as the possibilities sunk in.

"Do you have any other reason to expect something might have happened?" Gwen asked. "Any warning signs?"

Annie shook her head. "Not really. Alice sounded very excited on every call. But she did say the local people weren't very friendly."

"Did anyone threaten them?" Mary Beth asked.

"Not as far as Alice said," Anne admitted. "She might not have told me if they had though. She wouldn't have wanted me to worry."

"This island ... ," Stella said. "Was there anything dangerous about it?"

Annie explained about the legend associated with the island and the video they'd seen online. "But Alice said they hadn't seen any sign of dogs—nor heard any either." Then she told them about the satellite photos they'd looked at online.

"Oh my," Mary Beth said. "Those buildings sound dangerous."

"Do you think Jim and Alice might be hurt on the island somewhere?" Peggy asked.

"The thought had crossed my mind," Annie admitted. "But a lot of thoughts have crossed my mind in the last two days—crazy townspeople, vicious smugglers, demon dogs."

"I probably wouldn't worry much about demon dogs," Stella said drily. Then she looked around the group. "I really only see one answer to this."

"What's that?" Annie asked.

"We go down to South Carolina and see what's going on."

"Stella—don't you think that's a little extreme?" Gwen asked. "By the way, has anyone checked the weather down there? If there'd been a storm, that could account for no communication."

Annie looked at her in surprise. "You know, I hadn't thought to check on that."

"Well, that would be simple enough," Mary Beth said. "My laptop is in the back. We can just look it up."

"I'll get it," Kate offered, hopping up from her seat to hurry into the back.

"I'm not sure I would worry less," Annie said. "Thinking about Alice and Jim on an island during some horrible storm isn't very comforting."

"But it would give you an idea about what might be the problem," Mary Beth said.

Kate carried the computer to the shop counter. All the women stood around Mary Beth as she checked online newspapers on the South Carolina coast. None reported any kind of storm damage or power outages. "I guess it wasn't a storm," Mary Beth said.

"Then it's settled," Stella said. "We should go down there at once."

Gwen shook her head. "I'll have to pass on this road trip. John would worry worse than Annie."

"And I can't get away from work," Peggy said sadly. "Though I agree that someone needs to go check on her."

"Well, I'll go," Stella said firmly.

Mary Beth smiled. "If Kate doesn't mind staying behind to man the store, I'll drive us."

Annie held up a hand. "Well, before we plan a road trip, Ian said he'd track down all the local inns and have Chief Edwards call around. It may be that he can solve this mystery long-distance, and we'll get a call from Alice right away."

"Do you really believe that?" Stella asked skeptically.

"I'd like to."

"It does sound like we should wait to see what Ian's efforts produce," Mary Beth said. "But I'll be ready."

Peggy sighed. "I bet it's lovely and warm still in South Carolina."

"We're not going down to sunbathe," Stella said sternly.

"Unless we find Alice right away," Mary Beth added with a grin. "In which case, it would be a shame to waste the drive down."

Stella just shook her head in disapproval.

Annie felt a surge of affection and gratitude for all her friends. She was so glad she didn't have to face all her worry alone. She had to admit though, she would be happiest of all if she got home and found an email from Alice on her computer.

"I should head home," she said. "Oh, I missed nearly the whole Hook and Needle Club meeting. Is there anything I should know?"

"Just that we're on for the joint effort with the ladies at the Seaside Hills Assisted Living facility. Joan McTavish said they're very excited about it. How's your afghan going?"

"Amazingly well," Annie said. "Not only has the cool weather kept me indoors crocheting, but it's the only thing that can help calm me when I'm worried. So I've accomplished a lot in the past two days."

"I can just imagine Annie's flying crochet hook," Peggy said. Then she sighed. "Well, as always, I need to run." She gave Annie a quick hug. "Try not to worry too much. I'm sure it'll all turn out OK."

Annie smiled back. "Thanks, Peggy." Peggy tugged on a jacket over her waitress uniform and hurried out. As Annie watched her leave, she hoped fervently that Peggy's reassurances proved prophetic.

When Annie got home, she considered working off some of her nervous energy by raking the day's blanket of leaves. Alice often teased her about raking almost every day throughout October in a desperate attempt to keep the lawn neat. It was as if the New England winds conspired with the trees to drop just enough leaves each day to trigger her "I need to rake" mode.

"I'd rather wait until the trees are bald," Alice had told her once. "Then I just hire someone from the high school to rake them all up. Besides, they look pretty on the grass."

"Won't they kill the grass?" Annie had fretted.

"I expect the snow that's waiting around the corner will take care of the grass," Alice had said.

Annie looked over the fallen leaves again, but decided she'd better head into the house. She wanted to see if Alice had emailed. And she wanted to be close to the phone when Ian called with news of what he'd discovered.

Her computer had several emails, but all were trying to sell her something. With a sigh, she deleted them. She sat on the couch and pulled out her crocheting, hoping the feel of the yarn in her hands would calm her. Boots hopped up on the couch and climbed into her lap, nosing aside Annie's hands to make room.

Annie smiled at the gray cat. "Don't let me get in your way, Boots," she said wryly.

Boots simply curled up and closed her eyes. Annie had

been crocheting for about an hour when the phone rang. She jumped up so fast that Boots tumbled right out of her lap onto the floor.

"Sorry, Boots," Annie said as she lunged for the phone. "Ian?"

"Sorry, Mom, it's me."

Annie sank into the chair beside the phone. "No need to be sorry, darling. I was just expecting a call from Ian."

"Ian?" LeeAnn asked. "Should I call back?"

Annie was tempted to agree, but then she knew she was being ridiculous. She had call waiting. If Ian called, she would know. "No, but if my phone does that clicking thing, I'll need to switch calls," Annie said, apologetically.

"Wow!" LeeAnn said, her voice dropping to a whisper. "Is this getting serious?"

"Oh no, nothing like that," Annie stammered. "He's checking on something for me." Then to move the subject away from her love life, she quickly asked, "Have the twins decided on a pet yet?"

"No," LeeAnn said with a laugh. "And from the intensity of the *discussion*, we may be pet-free for a *long* time."

"At least they're learning debate skills from this," Annie said.

"Right, but let's get back to this call you're waiting for. What's Ian checking on? Not another mystery?" LeeAnn asked suspiciously. She was often less than enthusiastic about Annie's involvement in her more dangerous activities. Annie smiled a little at the thought—it was something LeeAnn and Ian had in common. They both thought Annie should be more careful.

"Well, not another mystery with me at the center," Annie said, and then she told her daughter about Alice and her disappearance, finishing with, "Alice wouldn't want to worry me like this."

"That does sound a little ominous," LeeAnn said. "I hope it turns out to be something simple like she lost her phone over the side of the boat, or they've been staying on the island for some reason or another."

"That sounds simple," Annie said with a laugh. "Anyway, enough about my fretting. You must have called to tell me something. If it's not a new pet decision, what's up?"

"Yes," LeeAnn said. "Joanna and John's school is putting together a talent show, and the twins have decided to be in it. They want to do an act together."

"How wonderful!" Annie said. "What kind of act?"

"Ah, that's the problem. Joanna wants to sing. And John wants to do magic. So they're in a minor battle to convince each other."

"Sounds dramatic," Annie said. "Was it a most intense discussion?"

"Definitely." LeeAnn laughed. "Right now I've declared a mandatory truce just so I can have a few minutes of peace. I figure I've got thirty minutes, tops."

"Well, whatever they decide to do, I'm sure it'll be wonderful," Annie said. "You'll have to video it for me."

"I will," LeeAnn said, and then Annie heard a crash and a shout in the background. "Oh, looks like the truce is over early. I'll talk to you later, Mom."

Annie was laughing as she hung up. She'd always been a little sad that LeeAnn never had any siblings, but the twins reminded her of how interesting life can get with more than one child.

Annie walked back to the sofa to find that Boots had hopped into her spot, directly on top of Annie's crocheting. When Annie tried to lift the sleepy cat, Boots clung to the afghan with her claws. Annie held the cat in one arm while she carefully picked each claw loose from the yarn.

"Thanks for reminding me that I still have a spoiled kid to deal with," Annie muttered as Boots tightened her grip on the afghan. Finally, she separated cat and crochet, and deposited Boots on the floor. The cat glared at her before beginning the dainty process of smoothing down her mussed-up fur.

Annie looked over the afghan, relieved to see that Boots hadn't done any damage, though she had added a lot of cat hair. Sitting back, Annie again lost herself in the smooth movement of the hook and the feel of the yarn in her fingers. At the speed she was going, she would have the piece done by the end of the week.

The crunch of tires on gravel pulled Annie out of her reverie. She looked toward the windows and realized night was falling. Annie tucked her afghan into her project bag to keep Boots from adding any more fur to it. Then she walked to the front door in time to hear a knock.

She pulled open the door and found Ian.

"Oh," she said. "I wasn't expecting a visit. I thought you'd just call."

Ian smiled. "I hope a visit isn't imposing."

"No, no," Annie said, backing away and gesturing for

Ian to come in. "You're always welcome, Ian. I hope you know that."

"I always like to hear it."

"Do you have anything new on Alice?" Annie asked.

Ian shook his head. "We called every hotel, motel, and inn within at least an hour's drive of Preacher's Reach. None of them have a record of Alice MacFarlane or Jim Parker staying there."

"That doesn't make sense," Annie said. "Alice told me they were at an inn, and it was local. She said it was hard to get a room because the locals seemed very unfriendly. And I could see behind her in the chat. She was definitely in a nice room."

Ian nodded. "Is there any chance they went to some other photo-shoot location and were going to Fuller's Island later?"

Annie shook her head. "No. Alice was very clear. She wouldn't have lied about that. There's no reason. Alice is a grown woman and could go wherever she liked."

"Then clearly someone else is lying," Ian said. "Someone is covering up Alice and Jim's stay."

"But why? They aren't government spies or anything crazy like that. Jim was just taking pictures of old buildings."

"I agree; it doesn't make any sense."

Annie took a deep breath. "I'm going down there."

"What?" Ian's eyebrows shot up so high Annie half expected them to hop off his head. "You're going to a hostile town that's covering up Alice's whereabouts. Since when does that sound like a good idea?"

"I'm not going alone," Annie said. "Mary Beth and

Stella are coming too. We're going to find out what happened to Alice. It's pretty clear that *something* has happened."

"Mary Beth and Stella?" Ian said. "Well, *that* makes me feel a lot better."

"I don't see any call for sarcasm," Annie said, feeling her temper rise.

"And I don't see any call for the three of you to rush off into danger," Ian said. "Do you really want to put an old woman like Stella in danger?"

Annie felt a pang of remorse, but only said, "Stella may be the toughest one of us all."

"That's not comforting," Ian said. "The woman is eighty-three years old."

"But she always has a knitting needle," Annie said. "Those things can be deadly."

"That's not funny," Ian answered, but a smile tugged at the corner of his mouth.

"Ian, I have to do something. I'm worried to death about Alice, and it's clear that she's not just off on a romantic adventure."

Ian nodded. "You're right. We need to go down and check it out."

"We?"

"I'm not going to let you go without me."

Annie frowned. "I'm not sure I need your permission."

Ian clearly saw where the conversation was going, and he held up his hand. "You know that's not what I meant. Look, I'll feel better if I come along. And you'll all be safer. It's a win for everyone."

"Won't you be missed, *Mr. Mayor?*" Annie asked.

"The tourists are thinning down, and I think Stony Point can survive without me for a few days," Ian said. "You're clearly intending to go down there whether I come or not. And I'm definitely not going to let you go alone."

"Not alone," Annie said.

"Alone with Mary Beth and Stella."

Annie had to admit, she would feel safer with Ian along, but she wasn't sure how Mary Beth and Stella would feel about it. "I need to ask the others," Annie said, hesitantly.

"As long as they know I *am* going."

Annie assumed that kind of attitude would go over about as well with Stella as it did with her. "I'll talk to them tomorrow." Then Annie laid a hand on Ian's arm. "I do appreciate your offering to come. I'm so worried about Alice."

"When did you intend to leave?" Ian asked.

"I'm not sure," Annie said. "We talked about it today at the Hook and Needle Club, but we didn't set a date because I wanted to wait until I heard from you."

Ian nodded. "I'll have to take care of some things at the office and put Tartan in the kennel. I would have Todd watch him, but the last time I left him with Todd, he took Tartan out on the boat, and Tartan ate a lobster. The result wasn't pretty."

Annie was sure Ian's brother had meant well. Todd always struck her as much more impulsive than Ian. Ian was anything but impulsive. Normally he planned everything, but here he was offering to just up and go to South Carolina. "You know, this seems a little out of the ordinary for you."

Ian raised an eyebrow. "I don't understand. You know you can count on me."

Annie shook her head. "Not that. It's the impulsiveness of it."

Ian smiled a little. "I've found I've become considerably more impulsive since I met you, Annie Dawson. I have to stay on my toes just to keep up with the predicaments you find yourself in."

"Well, this time it looks like Alice is the one in a predicament," Annie said.

Ian's face darkened. "And not surprisingly, I'll bet you that Jim Parker is at the center of it."

"You know Jim wouldn't want anything to happen to Alice," Annie reminded him again.

Ian relented reluctantly. He just nodded. "I should go. I need to get some things in order before the trip. Try not to worry too much. It won't help Alice if you don't sleep or eat between now and when we find her."

Annie agreed quietly. After Ian left, Annie stood for a few minutes on the porch, the chilly October breeze making her shiver. She looked out into the darkness. *Where are you, Alice?*

— 6 —

One of the servants on the island was an old woman we called simply "Cook"—she worked in the kitchen. By worked, I mean that she sat perched on a stool and commanded the kitchen staff with a sharp tone. She was tremendously old. Her eyes were so sunken into the many wrinkles of her face that I was certain she had no real eyes—but empty sockets shadowed by her heavy brows. She must have known we children were afraid of her because she took advantage of it, making strange magical signs with her hands if we lingered too long in the kitchen.

—Steven Fuller, 1925

Mary Beth and Stella were both happy to have Ian joining them for the trip to South Carolina—although Annie did have to take some ribbing from Mary Beth and Kate when she dropped by A Stitch in Time to run it by them. As it turned out, Stella was in the shop picking out yarn for a new project, so Annie was able to ask both at once about Ian coming along.

"Now I'm really concerned about Alice and Jim," Kate said, when the teasing wound down. "It's very unsettling that Ian couldn't find out where they'd stayed."

Annie nodded. "I agree. And I thought I was worried *before* Ian told me that, but why would an inn hide that information?"

"Well, maybe the people at the inn feel like they're protecting Jim and Alice's privacy," Kate said, but her voice didn't sound like she put much hope in that idea.

"I suspect the inn must have something to do with their disappearance," Stella said matter-of-factly. "Perhaps Jim and Alice discovered an extra mystery at the inn, and someone decided to keep them quiet."

Annie laid a hand on her stomach. Nerves had her twisted into knots.

"I don't think it's a good idea to speculate too wildly," Kate said as she looked anxiously at Annie. She reached out and squeezed Annie's arm. "You might find the answer really quickly once you get there."

Stella snorted, but she didn't offer any more bleak theories.

"I can wrap things up here and leave Friday morning," Mary Beth said. "I wish I could do it sooner, but I have something I must attend to tomorrow."

"I understand," Annie said. "I'll let Ian know. I don't know how soon he will be free either, but it would be wonderful if we could go soon."

"For you?" Kate said. "I expect he'd leave today."

"That seems unlikely," Annie said. "He is mayor, and he certainly always seems busy with the work of looking after Stony Point."

"Call Ian now," Stella commanded. "Let's get this settled. If we're leaving Friday morning, I need to move some appointments." She held up a hand before Annie could speak. "It's not a problem. At my age, it's mostly a matter of postponing perfectly unnecessary doctor appointments for a few days."

"If you're sure," Annie said doubtfully.

"I am sure."

Annie fished her phone out of her purse and found Ian's number on the speed dial. He answered on the second ring. "Annie! I hope you slept last night."

"Some," she said. "I'm here at A Stitch in Time. Mary Beth and Stella can leave Friday morning. They want to know if you can do that."

"I can," Ian said. "Listen, I'm tied up here for another hour. Can we meet for lunch after that?"

"To talk or to make sure I'm eating?"

"Both," Ian said with a chuckle. "I'm multitasking."

"I'll be happy to have lunch with you." As Annie ended the call, she looked up to find Mary Beth, Kate, and even Stella smiling at her. She didn't even bother to try to fend off the teasing. "Ian will be ready to leave Friday morning."

"I thought he would," Stella said. "I believe this is definitely the best course of action. The people of the area are far more likely to tell the truth when spoken to face-to-face."

Annie definitely thought it likely that Stella could get a confession out of most people—she was easily the most intimidating lady in Stony Point. Again a wave of worry washed over her, and she could feel the prickle of tears. "They've been missing for so long," she whispered. "I just hope they're all right."

Stella leaned forward so she was close enough for Annie to see the traces of powder in the creases of her face. "We're going to find them. I'm sure of it, and I'm rarely wrong about this sort of thing."

"We just have to keep the faith," Mary Beth said.

Annie nodded and managed a watery smile. "I'll try. I guess I'm a little tired."

"Did you sleep at all last night?" Mary Beth asked.

Annie shook her head. "Not much, really. Maybe I'll try warm milk tonight."

"You know, you might feel better if you stay busy," Mary Beth said. "Why don't you get Ian to tell you what inns are in that town. You can figure out which one we should stay at and make reservations."

Annie nodded. "I could do that."

"I'd like a room to myself," Stella said. She turned toward Mary Beth. "I don't tend to sleep many hours at a time, and I read at night. I wouldn't want to keep you up."

"No problem," Mary Beth said. "Do you want a roomie, Annie? I'm open." Then she grinned, her pixie smile full of mischief.

Annie nodded. "That would be fine. Unless you're planning to tease me endlessly. I may want a room as refuge."

"No teasing once we get going," Mary Beth said. "Well … not much anyway. Not unless I'm incredibly provoked. Oh dear, maybe you should get your own room. I just can't make any promises about my self-control."

Kate leaned over the counter and added. "Really, Annie, get your own room. She has been relentless in teasing me about Peter Matthews."

Annie didn't doubt that. Kate had spent most their drive home from the Texas needlecraft convention blushing. It was hard not to tease her over the handsome homicide detective who was clearly smitten with Kate, but Annie had mostly avoided the topic.

"Maybe I'd better just book four rooms," Annie said. "Unless I have to choose fewer, then I can room with Mary Beth and simply be brave. If we can find Alice and Jim right away, I'll be happy to be teased all the way home."

Everyone nodded in agreement about that. Mary Beth pulled a road atlas out from under the counter, and they all looked at it together to talk about the best route to Preacher's Reach.

"Don't you have a GPS?" Annie asked.

"Yes, but I don't like its bossy tone sometimes," Mary Beth said. "Beside, I like having a mental picture of the route."

The tinkle of the bell over the door drew their attention away from the maps. Ian Butler stepped through, his chocolate brown eyes as warm as his smile. Annie smiled back, feeling the knot in her stomach loosen the slightest bit. She was a little surprised at that feeling. She'd always had it with Wayne too—as soon as he walked in, any catastrophe seemed just a little bit more manageable. She'd never thought she would feel quite that trusting again.

"You ladies look very busy," Ian said.

"We're planning our route south," Mary Beth said.

"Oh?" Interest brightened his face still more, and he walked over to offer his own ideas about the route. Annie had always played map navigator when they drove long distances, but Wayne planned the basic route. It wasn't one of the things Annie found very interesting. She was always more focused on the actual arrival.

She stood back and watched her friends. Ian's neatly trimmed salt-and-pepper hair was almost a match to Mary

Beth's pixie cut of the same color. But beyond that, they had no similarity. Ian was tall and slender, towering over Mary Beth. While Mary Beth's face was pixie plump, Ian's was all angles and high cheek bones.

Kate and Stella were also a study in contrasts. Kate's shiny dark hair was cut above shoulder length, but long enough to swing forward and hide her face when she looked down. In contrast, Stella's perfect sweeps of soft gray hair wouldn't dare fall out of place. Both Stella and Kate stood taller than Mary Beth, which emphasized her elfin look.

Finally Ian tore himself away from the maps and turned toward Annie. "Ready for lunch?"

"I'm not very hungry," she admitted, "but I should try to eat something."

"I suspected as much," Ian said. "Maybe you could try a bowl of soup. It may be time for some comfort food."

They walked in companionable quiet to the diner. Peggy caught sight of them immediately and hurried across the room with a coffeepot clutched in one hand. "Any news of Alice?" she asked as soon as she reached them.

Ian shook his head. "We're going down to look for them."

"Oh." Peggy put a hand to her chest. "So you think something bad has happened too?"

Ian glanced at Annie, concern clearly showing on his face. Then he turned to Peggy. "We really don't know what has happened. But we're going to find out."

Peggy nodded. "Do you want a table near the windows or one more out of the way?"

Annie looked toward the lovely expanse of Town Square

that showed through the front windows from the angle where they stood. "I think I'd like to be near the window."

"Great—come this way." Peggy twirled with a swish of her pink uniform and headed back across the diner, weaving between tables with the ease of long experience.

Annie felt Ian's hand lightly on her back as he followed her. The tenderness of the gesture made Annie aware, once again, that her "just friends" assertion wasn't altogether honest. They were friends—good friends—but the hint of something more was always there. As the perfect mayor, Ian was concerned and protective of every person in Stony Point, but Annie would have to be totally blind not to see his feelings for her went deeper. And, even though Annie had told LeeAnn that her relationship with Ian wasn't getting serious, she realized it might well be.

As they sat, Peggy flipped their coffee cups over. "Coffee?" she asked. "Or do you want me to bring you some tea, Annie?"

Annie did find tea comforting, but she asked for coffee, hoping it would help shake some of the fog she was feeling from lack of sleep. Peggy poured expertly. "Are you two ready to order or do you need menus?"

"Soup," Ian said. "What kind do you have today?"

"Clam chowder," she said, "and a really nice hearty chicken noodle soup. It puts that nasty canned stuff to shame."

"Chicken noodle soup," Annie said. "I think I'm up for the ultimate comfort food today."

"Same for me," Ian agreed.

"Coming right up!"

Ian turned concerned eyes toward Annie. "How are you doing? At the risk of saying something that will trigger a fight, you look tired."

"I *am*," Annie said, "and a lot worried. But I'm glad that we're doing something. Knowing that I'm not going to sit helplessly at home with a cat in my lap, just hoping and praying for Alice to get back to me, helps."

"That does help," he agreed. "Just before I came to meet you, I talked to Chief Edwards. He's still looking for information about Alice and Jim. He called the police department at Preacher's Reach and finally someone remembered Jim."

"Oh?" Annie's eyes went wide. "Jim didn't get into any trouble, did he?"

"No, he just checked in at the department to let them know he had permission to go out to the island, since it was posted 'no trespassing.' And the police chief at Preacher's Reach told our Chief Edwards that the police station fielded a few calls from folks who apparently saw Alice and Jim's boat tied up at the island—again, folks calling in because the land is posted. Nothing serious."

"Oh well. That proves they got there," Annie said. "The video chat from Alice was from Preacher's Reach just like she said it was. It was starting to feel a little surreal when you couldn't find the inn where they were staying."

Ian nodded. "Chief Edwards asked the Preacher's Reach police chief to check into whether Jim and Alice's boat was still tied up at the island. He promised to send an officer out to see what he can find and get back to us."

"Good," Annie said. "If the boat is still there, they can search the island. Some of those buildings are old and decayed. They could be trapped in one and just need help getting out."

Ian nodded. "Who knows, they might be found even before we can get on the road."

A shiver ran up Annie's spine. "Of course, if they did get into some kind of accident on the island, they could be hurt. It isn't good that neither of them could make it back to the boat."

Ian held up his hand. "It could mean that, but it won't help them if we start imagining the worst."

"I have to admit, my imagination does that without much encouragement," Annie said.

Ian reached across the table and took Annie's hand, giving it a squeeze. "I've noticed," he said. "But you know, for all your wild mysteries and catastrophes, you and Alice have always come out just fine."

Annie smiled a little. They had been in more than one tight spot since she'd come to live in Stony Point. A couple of times, Annie had wondered if she was going to make it out of a mystery alive. She just hoped this particular adventure for Jim and Alice would work out as well.

Ian let go of Annie's hand discreetly as Peggy came back with two steaming crocks of soup. At the first taste, Annie realized she was hungry. Ian's report that the search for Alice wasn't just on hold until Friday was more comforting than she realized. She ate every drop of the delicious soup, and then sat back in the seat.

She realized Ian was grinning at her. "What?" she asked.

"I like a woman who doesn't feel like she has to eat like a bird," he said.

Annie blushed. "I guess I was hungrier than I thought."

"I'm just glad to see you eat," he said. "You need to keep up your strength."

Annie nodded. Who knew what kind of adventure lay ahead of them? She might need every bit of strength she could find.

— 7 —

*My female cousins were expected to keep clean and neat,
and stay indoors throughout our family visits to the island.
I felt bad for them—shut in the dark house that seemed to
sweat from invisible pores, so thick was the humidity. As
a boy, I was expected to spend my time out of doors where
my natural energy was less offensive to the grieving.
Considering the death of my great-grandfather to demon dogs
on the island, I found the outdoors less appealing than usual.
I wonder why no one felt that sending small boys to commune
with killer dogs was a bad idea.*

—Steven Fuller, 1925

Annie had expected the time to drag until they could leave
for South Carolina, but instead it flew by. Preparing for
the trip kept Annie busy. She pulled her summer
clothes out of the spare closet where she'd put them only a
few weeks before. She hadn't expected to see those things
for months. As she picked out outfits, she was careful to
keep in mind how much the temperature could change
on the Southern coast even at this time of year. Once the
sun went down, night often brought a chill. Annie picked
through blouses and sweaters, trying to choose things in the
more subdued shades of fall. The choosing helped dull some
of the worry that ate at her whenever she stopped moving.

Annie was surprised when Gwen called on Thursday, offering to drop by Grey Gables and check on Boots each day while Annie was gone. "I know Kate would do it," Gwen said, "but with her allergies, it just makes more sense for it to be me. And I live so close."

"I really appreciate that," Annie said. "I thought I might have to put Boots in a kennel, and I'm not sure she would ever forgive me for that."

Gwen laughed. "If I know cats, you'd certainly get the cold shoulder for a while."

With that concern out of the way, Annie finished packing for the trip. She added a few extra pairs of shoes and older, practical clothes since they were likely to be wading through the brush on Fuller's Island.

Late on Thursday, Ian finally called to let her know what Chief Edwards had found out. "Apparently the boat Jim and Alice were using is no longer tied up at the island," Ian said.

"Did they check the island anyway?" Annie asked.

"They said they did," Ian answered. "But Chief Edwards said he isn't sure they looked very hard since the boat was gone. I did find out where the boat came from."

"Oh, that's good!" Annie said hopefully.

"Maynard's Boats and Bait rented the boat to Jim," Ian said. "The owner told the police that the boat just turned back up at their dock. Since Jim had paid by credit card, they didn't think anything of it. They just assumed he turned it in after hours."

"So that's another dead end," Annie said sadly.

"Well, it's another end we're going to investigate when we get down there," Ian said. "I'm not so sure I'm taking anyone down there at their word—not after the chief couldn't find any inn that would admit to renting rooms to Alice and Jim. Who knows who else is lying?"

"I'm so worried," Annie said softly.

"I know better than to tell you not to worry," Ian said. "But remember, we're going down there. We're going to find them."

As with their past road trip, they planned to gather in the small parking lot behind A Stitch in Time. When Ian updated Annie on Chief Edwards report, he offered to pick her up Friday morning so her car wouldn't have to sit in the lot while they were gone.

"But what about your car?" Annie asked.

"I'm driving the truck. Todd is going to come and pick it up," Ian said. "He wanted to borrow it anyway to haul some lobster pots home for repairs. This will let him help me and get his chore done."

"Sounds like a plan then," Annie said, warmed again at how thoughtful her friends continuously were.

Then, suddenly, it was Friday morning and the alarm was going off in her pitch-dark bedroom. "The only thing wrong with an early start," Annie told her grumpy cat as she gently pushed Boots over enough to sit up, "Is that it means you have to wake up early."

Annie hurried through her shower, and then wandered through the house, checking that everything was secure. She'd already packed her laptop for the trip, but she had to fight the urge to log in again—just in case Alice had sent a message.

She was still checking that all her small appliances were unplugged when she heard the bite of Ian's tires in the gravel outside. As she walked to the front door, Boots wove between her legs, nearly tripping her twice.

"Boots!" Annie scolded. "You're not going to be any happier if I break my neck!"

She pulled open the front door, gently pushing the cat behind her. She didn't want Boots getting any ideas about dashing outside now—they'd never get started on time if she had to look for an escaped cat.

"You ready?" Ian asked when the door was open enough to see him.

"Just about," Annie said. "Come on in. Boots is in a mood."

"I thought cats were always in a mood," Ian said.

"Mostly," Annie said with a sigh. "But on the upside, she's a good cuddler, and she keeps my feet warm at night."

Ian opened his mouth to say something, his eyes sparkling, but then seemed to think better of it. Instead he bent down to rub Boots's ears. The cat caught one sniff of Ian's hands and backed away, her hair fluffed out.

Ian and Annie looked at each other. "Tartan!"

"I wish they could be friends," Ian said. "Tartan would like Boots … after he chased her around a little."

"He might not like her claws so much," Annie answered. "Boots has a history of dealing with anyone she sees as a trespasser."

"That's for sure," Ian said. He looked around the room, and then headed over to pick up Annie's suitcase. "Is this all you're bringing?"

"Not quite," Annie said. She walked to the sofa and picked up her purse, crochet project bag, and laptop bag. "I come with accessories."

"You still travel light," Ian said. "I admire that."

"Hopefully it won't mean I spend half the trip thinking of things I wish I'd brought," Annie told him.

Ian smiled. "Anything else? Are we ready?"

Annie looked around once more. "I guess." Then she squared her shoulders and said more decisively, "Yes, I'm ready. I checked the house, and I'm not going to worry about anything I might have left undone."

"Good girl." Ian said, turning to head for the door. "Let's go."

Annie scooped up Boots just as the cat was ready to make her move on the open door. She backed through the door after Ian, and then shoved the cat back inside and pulled the door closed.

"You know," Ian said. "The kennel is really a very nice place."

"I'm sure it is," Annie agreed. "But Boots would rather be home, and Gwen said she'd check on her."

Ian raised his eyebrows. "That's nice of her. Did you warn her she might get cat hair on her clothes?"

"Gwen isn't that obsessive about her clothes," Annie said. "Besides, I left a clothes brush on the table by the door."

Ian put Annie's suitcase in the bed of the truck beside his own, and then he opened the door for her. "Do you want me to put any of those in the back?" he asked, nodding toward the bags in her hands.

"No, I can hold them." Annie stepped up into the truck, settling the bags around her feet.

As they arrived at the parking lot, they saw Stella's

driver, Jason, pull the sparkling white Lincoln in beside Mary Beth's SUV. Kate leaned against the back of the SUV beside Mary Beth.

When Ian pulled up close, Annie hopped out, not wanting him to feel like he had to come around and open her door. She headed toward her friends. "Kate! Did you change your mind? Are you coming with us?"

Kate shook her head. "No, just seeing you off. I knew Mary Beth would have last-minute things to tell me, and I thought I would save her a phone call."

"I only had a couple," Mary Beth said.

Jason carried Stella's two suitcases to the SUV. "Would you like me to pack the suitcases into the SUV again?" At the start of their last road trip, Jason had proved he was an expert at the tricky job of luggage Tetris.

"Be my guest," Mary Beth said. "It should be a little easier since I don't have boxes of needlework this time."

Jason took Ian and Annie's bags and quickly placed everything neatly in the back of the SUV. He even tucked in Annie's laptop where it could be easily reached if she wanted to pull it out at a meal stop.

"Excellent as always, Jason," Stella said.

"Thank you." The tall man smiled fondly at Stella. Then he nodded at each person and headed back to the Lincoln.

"Wow," Mary Beth said. "He didn't nag you about anything."

"We had a little talk after last time," Stella said.

"Meaning he probably nagged her before they got here," Mary Beth said.

"I believe I said what I meant," Stella said firmly.

"So who wants to ride shotgun since Kate isn't coming?" Mary Beth asked.

Stella sniffed. "Though I dislike that phrase, I would enjoy sitting up front with you." She turned toward Ian and Annie. "If neither of you mind?"

"Not at all," Ian said. "But you have to let me help drive when you get tired."

"Oh, don't worry, I will," Mary Beth said.

Finally, quick hugs were exchanged with Kate, and the travelers piled into the car and started the journey. As Ian folded into the seat beside her, Annie realized just how long-legged her friend was. "I bet you have fun on planes," she said.

"Sure. I like it when I can look at my knees up close. I actually try not to fly much, and then I usually spring for first class."

"I can see why you'd need to," she said. "Though I would probably feel too decadent."

"What part of that makes you feel decadent?" Ian asked her. "The tiny pillow or the really bad food?"

Annie laughed. "OK, my natural frugality would prevent me." She turned and looked out the side window. "I wish now that I'd checked my email this morning."

"You could check it on your phone," Ian suggested.

"Really?" Annie said in surprise. "I wouldn't know how."

"Let me see your phone, and I'll walk you through it," he said. "You don't want to send a lot of emails with your phone though. Those tiny keyboards are painful."

Ian scooted a bit closer to Annie as he held up the phone to show her the process of checking her email. In the slightly chilly car, she could feel the warmth coming from him and resisted the urge to lean into him for comfort. She had to give herself a little inner shake to focus on his explanation.

She answered his questions about her email account and watched as he seemed to magically bring up her email on the small phone screen. There was nothing from Alice; LeeAnn sent a short email wishing her luck on the trip and telling her to be safe.

The rest of the emails were either trying to sell her something or targeting greedy and gullible people with one scam or another. Ian frowned. "You should probably get a spam filter."

"I just delete them," Annie said. "My son-in-law told me about all the emails to avoid. So really, I don't read most of what comes in my box."

"That's good," Ian said as he closed her email and handed the phone back to her. Then he leaned toward her slightly more, so he could look out the window beside her.

Annie smiled. "Did you want *this* window seat?"

Ian sat back up. "Sorry. Actually I have more leg room here."

The morning hours passed pleasantly, and eventually, Annie grew used to having Ian look over her to peer out the window now and then. When they finally stopped for lunch, he offered to drive for a while.

"You should let him," Annie said as she stirred cream into her coffee. "He'll enjoy looking out the nice big window."

Ian grinned sheepishly. "Sorry, I'm a terrible rider. Todd

always says it's like driving with a dog in the car. I just can't seem to sit still when I'm not driving."

Mary Beth coughed into her hand, only half-hiding the words "control freak."

Ian laughed aloud at that. "Maybe a little."

"Personally, I've never had an interest in driving," Stella said. "I find I enjoy the ride more when I don't pay attention to the other cars on the road."

"That would be a hindrance to driving," Mary Beth said with an impish smile.

"I don't mind driving," Annie said. "Especially at night. I like the quiet of night driving."

"I did when I was younger," Mary Beth admitted. "But as my eyes get older, I find I have to stay on my toes when I drive at night. I don't find that relaxing."

"I don't mind night driving," Ian told them. "But I dislike storm driving."

Their driving talk was interrupted when the server brought their order, and they all tucked hungrily into lunch. As she chewed, Annie glanced out the window at the bright day. They were making good time on the road, but she wished they could go faster. *Alice, where are you?*

— 8 —

We didn't normally spend much time on the mainland when we visited my great-grandparents. Mainland children were considered unacceptable playmates to a member of the Fuller family. After my great-grandfather's death, my mother took every chance to leave the oppressive mourning on the island and spend time on the mainland. She always took me with her. Father didn't like that, but Mother was a difficult woman to refuse.

—Steven Fuller, 1925

They didn't stop for the night until far later than the women in the car might have chosen. Ian had kept his spot as driver for the rest of the day, and he never seemed to get tired. Finally, Stella simply demanded he find a place for the night so she could get out of the car and lie down.

The hotel was simple but clean. Annie and Mary Beth shared a room since they were both nearly ready to fall asleep on their feet. Annie didn't care who she spent the night with at that point—as long as she got to lie down and sleep.

She quickly discovered that Mary Beth snored. The snorts and rumbles couldn't keep Annie awake long though, and she slept through the night without interruption. The next morning, they rushed through the small breakfast that the hotel offered and got back on the road while the moon still hung pale and ghostly in the brightening morning sky.

The second day passed quickly. Ian offered to drive at breakfast, and then turned down any invitations to switch off. Everyone felt the urgency of getting there and finding Alice. Throughout the drive, it was like watching autumn undo itself. In Maine, most of the color was passing, and a number of the trees had dropped all their leaves, though enough stubborn limbs held out to keep homeowners raking. However, as they drove south, trees held more and more leaves. That sense of going back in time was so strong that Annie wished they really were—going back to the time before she had ever shown Jim that book and sent her best friend into trouble.

"We should probably check into our rooms before we do anything else," Ian said, interrupting Annie's thoughts.

"OK," Annie said. "Why?"

"Well, Alice said they had trouble getting anyone to rent them a room, right?" Ian darted the look toward Annie, before putting his attention back on the road. "It seems wise to get settled before we start annoying people."

Annie smiled faintly. "That's probably wise since I plan to be fairly annoying."

Ian laughed. "I would gallantly say that is unlikely, but you certainly can be stubborn when you're after something."

Annie crossed her arms. "Tenacious."

"Right, that's the word I meant."

Annie, who moved to the front seat when Ian was driving, looked out the wide expanse of windshield. That was one of the perks of riding in Mary Beth's SUV—it felt like you could see the whole world. The highways were busier than Annie had expected for so late in the year, and she was glad she wasn't driving.

"Will it still be light when we get to Preacher's Reach?" Stella asked.

"Should be," Ian answered. "We got an early start today."

"I hope you're still planning to let us out of this thing for lunch," the matriarch of the group said. "I'm all for getting there, but if we're so stiff we can't move, it'll be hard to pull off a daring rescue once we find Alice and her friend."

Annie smiled as she imagined Stella pulling off a daring rescue any time. Although intimidating in her own way, she wasn't exactly athletic. Then she wrung her hands in worry. Other than Ian, were any of them really capable of daring rescues?

She felt Ian's warm hand on her arm. "It's going to be OK," he said.

"You can't know that," she said.

"I can feel it," Ian told her, "and I believe it."

I wish I could, Annie thought, but she gave Ian's hand a pat and nodded. The she turned her head slightly away from him, as if engrossed in something in the landscape that flashed by.

Ian navigated the busy traffic well, and they were all grateful not to get caught in any real traffic jams. The highway was busy but moving, and they made such good time that even stopping for lunch didn't change Ian's optimistic hopes of reaching their destination before dark.

As the hours passed, they moved deeper and deeper into the South. Annie began to recognize patches of kudzu, the amazing plant that seemed intent on burying the entire

South in green. At one spot, she saw a power pole that had been cleared of kudzu at the base, but a clump still clung to the top of the pole as if it had climbed up there and now crouched on the crossbeam, looking down on the passing traffic. Soon after they left Virginia, they passed a stand of trees completely covered by kudzu as if someone had thrown a thick green blanket over the landscape.

"What is that plant?" Stella asked.

"Kudzu."

"Oh, I've heard of that," Mary Beth said. "I'm surprised they let it get so out of hand."

"I understand it takes a lot of work to keep it under control," Annie said. "And on roadsides, they don't always put in the time and money."

"Do you suppose we'll see any of that on the island?" Mary Beth asked.

"I saw a lot of thick growth in the satellite photos," Annie said. "But with it being an island and isolated, I think it's likely to have more native growth."

As she spoke, she saw Ian's facial expression change, as if he'd had a disturbing thought. Annie leaned slightly closer to him and said, "You look upset."

He forced a smile. "I just had a thought about plants."

"Oh?"

"Well, Fuller's Island is remote," he said. "I just wondered if that might be what Alice and Jim stumbled into."

"What?" Annie asked, completely confused.

"A grow site," Ian said, glancing at her. "What if someone is using the island's overgrowth to hide an illegal marijuana grow site? They certainly would be upset if Alice and Jim walked in on it. And they might keep dogs to chase people away."

Annie's eyes grew wide. "Drugs? You think it might be drugs?" She sat back as fresh fear washed over her. Who knew what could have happened if her friends walked in on drug growers?

"It was just a thought," Ian said. "Look, I'm probably way off track. After all, the police sent someone out to look for Alice and Jim on the island. Surely a search would have turned up fields of marijuana plants if they were there."

"Oh, right," Annie said, her voice breathy with relief. "Of course they would."

"I hear whispering up there," Mary Beth said. "Want to share with the class?"

"Ian had a thought about Fuller's Island being used as a marijuana growing site," Annie said. "But the police would have seen that when they looked for Alice and Jim."

"Unless the police are in on it," Stella said.

"Don't you think that's just a *little* paranoid?" Mary Beth asked.

Stella shrugged. "I've seen movies."

"I've seen movies with aliens and talking dogs too," Mary Beth said. "But I don't think they're involved here."

Stella made a harrumph sound but offered no more comment.

"The island could be involved in smuggling," Mary Beth said. "Even Stony Point has had its history with smugglers."

"I had considered that," Ian said. "And Chief Edwards specifically asked about smuggling. He said he may have offended the police chief in Preacher's Reach, but they were adamant that they do not have a smuggling problem."

"I'd imagine smugglers try to keep their activities quite secret from the police," Stella said.

"Apparently the island is fairly hard to reach from the ocean side because of some dangerous rocks," Ian said. "And planes would be spotted—the island isn't that far from shore. I don't think it would be ideal for smuggling."

Annie was glad smuggling was unlikely. The thought of Alice and Jim tangling with dangerous criminals made her stomach hurt. Still, clearly something had happened to them.

After that, they fell again to thinking their own thoughts as they hurried down the coast. It was early afternoon when they finally crossed the border into South Carolina, and soon they left the interstate and began following the GPS directions to find the small coastal town.

"This is definitely not one of the more touristy areas," Mary Beth said as they passed houses and small businesses that looked tired and well-battered by weather and years. The buildings were small with pale siding and metal roofs.

"I suspect it's too swampy," Ian said.

One squat building that looked like it was both home and business had a hand-lettered sign near the road offering "boiled peanuts."

"Oh, that sounds disgusting," Mary Beth said.

"I've never had them," Annie admitted, "but Wayne liked them. He tried them first on a trip to the Southeast, and then he found some online source to get them shipped to him. I never could get myself to taste them, though he always tried to coax me into it. It just doesn't sound very appealing."

The narrow state roads forced them to drive more slowly, though the roads weren't busy. Here and there, huge tree limbs dripping with Spanish moss reached toward the road. The appearance of well-tended gas stations and convenience stores suggested they were getting close to the town.

More and more small shops appeared; many had the short palmetto trees planted nearby in groups of two or three. They passed the magistrate's office, one of the few brick buildings. The volunteer fire department was attached, its tall garage doors closed.

"I'm beginning to think of Stony Point as shockingly urban," Mary Beth said.

Not far down the road, they came to a cinder-block building that housed *The Preacher's Reach News* office. The concrete platform and capped pipes out front that showed the newspaper office had once been a gas station. Behind the news office, another small block building wore a sign for the historical society.

After that, most of the buildings were homes, though bigger and better kept than the ones they'd passed earlier. Annie glanced down at the GPS and saw they were nearly at the B&B where they had reservations. It was called The Preacher's Rest.

"We turn right just ahead," Annie said.

"OK." Ian scanned the road for the turn. The road itself was unmarked.

Finally, they spotted the inn. It was a two-story, white building with a porch that covered the front of the house and swept around to one side. The white wicker chairs on the porch reminded Annie of Grey Gables. A half-round drive paved with brick connected with the road on each end. The front porch steps led directly to the highest point in the curve. Off to the side of the old house, Annie saw a small parking lot. It only held one car. Huge old, twisted trees stood near the house, dripping with moss and giving the place an ancient look. Behind the house, more trees hung over a few small outbuildings, and beyond that lay an overgrown field.

"Looks nice," Mary Beth said.

Ian pulled carefully into the small parking lot, and everyone climbed out. Annie looked at the house as she stretched. She saw Stella was limping a bit from the stiffness of the long ride and hoped the inn had plenty of hot water. She suspected they would all benefit from a hot soak.

Ian began handing out luggage from the back of the SUV, carrying his own and one of Stella's bags. Annie slipped the long handles of her small bags over her shoulder and started toward the inn, pulling her wheeled suitcase behind her.

A tiny woman with snow-white hair, pulled back and braided into a long plait, stepped out on the porch to welcome them. "Welcome to the Preacher's Rest. Are you the Dawson party? I hope you found us without too much difficulty," she said.

"We did," Ian answered. "GPS is one of the greatest inventions of the modern world."

"It's good," the woman agreed. "But it takes the fun out of getting good and lost. You miss out on so many surprises."

"After all that driving," Stella said, "I don't think I have the energy for many surprises."

"Well, I have your rooms for you," she told them. "You'll have the whole second floor to yourselves. We only have two downstairs rooms and only one of them is taken, so it should be nice and quiet for sleeping."

"That will be lovely," Stella said.

The lobby of the inn was small but sparkling clean and bright. A pleasant breeze came from each window. "We have air conditioning," the innkeeper said. "But we don't use it this time of year. There's always a breeze, but it won't really turn cold enough to close the windows for another month or so."

"This is a lovely place," Mary Beth said.

The woman's smile widened. "Thank you. It was built in the 1920s and has been in my family ever since, though it didn't become an inn until my husband and I remodeled. I'm Suzanne Ayers."

Everyone murmured greetings as Mrs. Ayers opened the guest registry for them to sign in. "We serve a brunch in the dining room each morning. On Sundays it's actually very popular with our neighbors, so you'll find the room quite busy then. But we'll hold a table just for your group."

"Thank you," Annie said.

Mrs. Ayers took Stella's bag from her and looked at Stella with some concern. "Do you think the stairs will be a problem for you?" she asked. "I could give you the empty downstairs room."

"I'm just a bit stiff from the drive," Stella answered regally. "I can climb stairs quite well."

Annie was delighted with her well-lit room. The carved cherry four-poster bed was covered with a lovely handmade quilt in shades of sage and terra-cotta. The walls of the room were painted in a matching sage. Carved cherry tables on either side of the bed held porcelain lamps with delicately tinted cherubs that made Annie smile. She wouldn't have wanted one of the lamps, but somehow, they suited the room.

The windows had simple mini blinds for their only window treatment, but the shades were up, and the windows open, bathing the room in soft light and sweet fresh air. Annie stood in the middle of the room and spun slowly. The room didn't really look much like what she'd seen behind Alice in the video chats, but something about it was the same.

She looked over the room again and realized it was the lack of window treatments. The room Alice had stayed in didn't have curtains either. Annie was sure of it. This wasn't Alice's room, but it might have been Alice's inn.

Annie stepped out of her room and knocked on the next door. Mary Beth opened the door. "Yes?"

"Do your windows have curtains?" she asked.

"No," Mary Beth said in surprise. "Why do you ask?"

"I think this might be the inn where Alice and Jim stayed," Annie said. "Can I see your room?"

Mary Beth nodded, stepping back to make room for Annie to walk in. The room was also charming though a bit smaller than Annie's. The walls were painted a lovely shade of cranberry. The bed was white with a snowy white coverlet. The white side table held a more modern-looking, black-and-white lamp that went well with the crisp lines of the bed.

Annie sighed. It was not the room she'd seen in Alice's chat.

"Let's check with the others," Mary Beth suggested.

Stella's room was about the size of Annie's with a white four-poster bed and a cream and rose quilt. The walls were a rosy taupe. It also had a white side table with a white porcelain lamp and Victorian shade.

"Not this one either," Annie said, beginning to wonder if she'd imagined the similarity between the windows of the rooms and the windows in Alice's video chat.

"There's still Ian's room," Mary Beth said.

Ian looked surprised at finding the three women standing in the hall outside his room. "Is there a problem?"

"Annie thinks this might be the inn that Alice and Jim stayed in," Mary Beth said.

"We need to check your room," Stella added.

Ian smiled and stepped back to let the group in. His room was the largest of the four, though only slightly. A huge four-poster cherry bed took up much of the space, with its matching highboy dresser. The windows of the room were taller than in the other three rooms and faced west.

Annie slumped slightly. "Not this room either. I guess I was wrong."

"Maybe not," Ian said. "Mrs. Ayers said there were two rooms downstairs. With Jim's limp and cane, I'm sure she offered one or both to Jim and Alice, just as she offered one to Stella."

"Now how are we going to get inside to see those downstairs rooms?" Mary Beth asked.

"Well, we could get one of them easily enough," Ian answered. "Stella just needs to decide the stairs are too much for her after all."

Stella made a face but agreed. "I suppose I can be frail for the cause."

They trooped downstairs. Ian carried both of Stella's bags. Mrs. Ayers was no longer in the front foyer, so Ian set the bags down beside the front desk as they split up to go looking for the woman.

Annie opened a pair of double French doors and found herself facing a bright dining room, but the innkeeper was not inside. She turned and walked down a short hall where a door stood partly open. Annie knocked gently as she pushed the door open further. Mrs. Ayers was pulling a crisp white pillowcase on one of the long bed pillows. She looked up and smiled at Annie. "Can I help you?"

"Stella found the stairs a bit more trying that she expected," Annie said, smiling back. "She tries so hard to be independent. Can she still switch to a downstairs room?"

"Of course," Mrs. Ayers said. "I'll meet you all at the front desk. I'm almost done here if you don't mind my finishing up."

"No, of course not," Annie said. "The rooms here are lovely."

"Thank you." Again the woman's smile warmed still more at the compliment.

Annie's eyes swept the room carefully before backing out. Like her room, it had cherry furniture. Like Ian's room, the windows were very tall. And like every room she'd seen so far, it was definitely not the room from Alice's chat.

"One more chance," Annie murmured to herself as she headed for the front desk. She found the others already grouped there.

"We couldn't find her," Ian said.

"I did," Annie told them. "She was cleaning the room that's in use. It wasn't the right room."

"Well, only one room left," Mary Beth said.

Mrs. Ayers soon joined them and quickly led them to Stella's new room. The room was painted a light yellow. The furniture was white with the big bed dominating the room. The headboard and footboard were beadboard panels and the quilt was in soft shades of lavender, green and yellow.

Annie gasped as they walked in. This had been Alice's room.

-9-

On one trip to the mainland, my mother stopped at a small dress shop to have a bit of lace repaired on her best traveling gloves. The shop smelled of dried roses as if the funeral flowers that filled the Fuller mansion had followed us with their ghostly scent. I found it boring as only a small boy could be bored—with every particle of my being. Eventually my mother grew annoyed enough by my fretsome behavior that she sent me out to play on the sidewalk in front of the shop to maintain her own sanity.

—Steven Fuller, 1925

After Mrs. Ayers left them alone in the room, Annie told the others about the room.

"You're sure?" Mary Beth asked.

Annie nodded. "Now that I see it again, it's very clear in my head. I remember seeing the beadboard panels behind Alice and the picture on the wall with the dog. I especially remember the dog because the whole reason for coming to South Carolina was because of ghost dogs."

"Are you sure Chief Edwards spoke to the innkeeper here?" Stella asked Ian.

"I don't know why he would miss this inn," Ian said. "Annie found it easily enough to make the reservations."

Mary Beth rubbed her hands together. "So, do we grill Mrs. Ayers?"

"Eventually," Ian said. "But right now, it might be better not to. I'd like to ask around at some businesses they may have visited, and I'd rather no one called ahead to warn people off."

"Great," Mary Beth said. "When do we start?"

"Now would be fine," Annie said. "The sooner we start, the sooner we find Alice."

"I don't believe I'm up for it," Stella said. "I'd like a nice hot soak and some rest before dinner. In fact, if you are all sleuthing into the dinner hour, you can bring me back a nice salad."

"We can do that," Annie agreed. "Are you OK?"

Stella nodded as she walked over to sit on the edge of the bed. "Just tired. We made our last road trip at a more leisurely rate."

"Lives weren't at stake the last time," Mary Beth said.

They left Stella to her rest and headed out to the parking lot. "Where to first, Mr. Mayor?" Mary Beth asked.

Ian smiled. "Is the 'Mr. Mayor' a hint that I'm being bossy?"

"No," Mary Beth said with a grin. "You can tell when you're being bossy. Smoke comes out of Annie's ears."

"It does not," Annie protested, then when her friends both turned to look at her, she relented a little. "I save that for when he's being overprotective."

"I won't apologize for caring."

Mary Beth stepped between them. "OK—back to the original question. Where to first?"

"I thought we'd stop by the police department," Ian said. "I programmed the address into the GPS at the hotel last night along with a few others. We may get more details there on what they're doing to find Jim and Alice."

"Sounds like a plan," Mary Beth said cheerfully, and then she quickly hopped into the back of the SUV, leaving Annie to ride in the front next to Ian.

"That is a good idea," Annie agreed as Ian opened the door for her.

The warmth in Ian's smile made Annie blush, even though she couldn't have said exactly why. They pulled out of the small parking lot and turned back onto the state road.

"So ... do we have a plan for the police department?" Mary Beth said. "Shall we go in like they do on television—good-cop, bad-cop? Because if we do, I want to be the bad cop."

Annie stifled a grin at the idea of tiny Mary Beth intimidating anyone, but Ian didn't even try to repress a chuckle. "I thought we'd just go in and introduce ourselves and ask questions."

Mary Beth sat back and crossed her arms. "Party pooper."

Ian grinned at her in the rearview mirror. "Maybe you can be the bad cop when we get back to the inn and grill Mrs. Ayers." That seemed to perk Mary Beth up considerably.

The GPS directions took them back the way they came, though they turned off the state road to reach the police station. The station was a squat white cinderblock building with a flagpole in front. A cracked walk led to double glass doors. Several windows faced the street, each with a small air conditioner dripping into the narrow bed that ran the length of the building. The bed held a row of exactly spaced, severely trimmed boxwoods and a lot of brown bark mulch. Taken together, the look was institutional and slightly depressing.

Inside was more of the same. The walls were half cheap, dark paneling and half cinder-block, painted an odd shade of green. The air inside was warm and felt thicker than the air outside. Ian walked to the front desk, pulling a notebook out of his pocket as he went. He introduced himself to the woman behind the desk and explained that he was following up on some calls Chief Edwards had made.

The woman looked at Ian sharply, reminding Annie for a moment of Ian's secretary Charlotte. Then she simply nodded and said, "Let me get the chief."

Several minutes later, the woman trailed back to her stool and a painfully thin, older man came through a door, holding out his hand. "I'm Chief Harper. You're lucky you caught me here; I'm usually home by now. I understand you're the mayor of Stony Point, Maine?"

"That's right," Ian said, shaking the man's outstretched hand. "And these are friends of the missing people. This is Annie Dawson, and this is Mary Beth Brock."

"I'm sorry to hear about your friends going missing," Chief Harper said. "I didn't actually talk to either of them." He turned to the woman on the stool. "You remember speaking to them though, don't you, Doris?"

Doris seemed unhappy at the question. "We aren't a big tourist area," she said. "So I don't get that many folks walking in—'specially not someone who looked like a hooligan and claimed to be a fancy book author."

Annie wasn't sure whether to be offended or amused by the woman's description of Jim. It did sound a lot like the way Stella talked about him, but somehow it sounded worse coming from a stranger.

"And he asked about Fuller's Island," Ian prompted.

The woman's frown darkened. "Yeah, he claimed to have permission to take pictures there. I wasn't sure. He wasn't real steady on his feet, and I thought he might have been drinking."

That helped convince Annie. Now she was insulted on Jim's behalf. "He's a little unsteady because he lost his legs in a hotel bombing in a war zone. He was a war correspondent."

The woman shrugged. "I didn't know that, did I?"

Ian cleared his throat for attention. "So, did you help Mr. Parker?"

"I sent him to talk to Leroy," the woman said.

The group turned back to Chief Harper. "One of my officers. He checks over the island now and again. Runs off the ghost hunters. He's the one who went out and looked for your friends."

"Could we talk to him?"

"I'd be happy to let you," Chief Harper said. "But Leroy had a family emergency and took some time off."

"Perhaps we could talk to him at home," Ian said.

"He's not at home," the Chief said. "The family emergency took him to Georgia. I don't have a number."

"How convenient," Mary Beth muttered.

"We filed a report after your chief called," Chief Harper said. "But honestly, you're talking about two adults who can do pretty much whatever they like. It sounds to me like they just changed their plans and didn't let the nosy neighbors back home know about it."

"That's because you don't know Alice and Jim," Annie said.

"If you did," Mary Beth added. "You wouldn't say anything so insulting."

Chief Harper and Doris both puffed up some at that, and Ian quickly spoke up. "Thank you both for your time. We'll be going out to the island to see if our friends left anything behind that might be meaningful to us. I have permission from the owner."

Annie looked at Ian in surprise. She hadn't known he'd spoken to the owner of the island.

"I wish you good luck," Chief Harper said, sounding as if he wished them anything but good luck. "Let me know if my officers can help you in any way."

"Actually, you can," Ian said. "You could let me know the name of a boat rental in the area."

"Rental?" Chief Harper said. "You know your way around a boat?"

"I come from a long line of lobstermen," Ian answered. "I was on a boat before I was on a bike."

The Chief exchanged a look with Doris. "I reckon you should try Maynard's Boats and Bait. He does some trade in tourist boat rentals."

"Do you have an address for that?" Ian asked.

"Look that up for the nice folks," Chief Harper said to Doris. He sounded a bit cheerier now that the interview was clearly winding down. "If y'all will excuse me, I need to finish up some paperwork. It's the bane of my existence."

"I know how that is," Ian told him.

The chief disappeared back through the door from which he'd first come. Doris grudgingly pulled out a skinny telephone book and looked up the boat rental address in the yellow pages. She scrawled something on one of the department business cards and handed it back. "You need directions?"

"No, thank you," Ian said. "We'll let you get back to your work."

He quickly ushered the women outside, where he pulled a pen from his pocket and quickly wrote on the card he held. When he finished, Annie looked at him quizzically. "I saw a few other boat rentals on the page Doris was checking," he said. "I thought I would write them down, just in case Maynard's is less than welcoming."

"Clever," Mary Beth said admiringly.

Ian looked up and down the street. Directly behind the police station, a whitewashed water tower looked down on them. More businesses lined the street further down. "Let's take a little walk and see if anyone remembers Alice and Jim."

They walked past the parking lot for the police department and soon reached a short row of brick storefronts: a hardware store, a small grocery, and a dry cleaner.

"I think we should divide and conquer," Mary Beth said. "We'll look less intimidating one at a time. I'll take the dry cleaner, and Ian should probably do the hardware store. It's a guy place."

"Hey," Annie said. "I've spent a lot of time in Malone's Hardware in Stony Point."

"Do you want the hardware store?" Ian said.

Annie shook her head. "Knowing Alice, the grocery is the most likely. She'd want snacks."

They divided and headed into the stores. The grocery was small with cramped aisles between metal rows of shelving. Cold storage lined the back and one side wall. The store was quiet except for the sound of the ceiling fan which wobbled slightly as it turned.

The store had two checkout stands, but only one was manned. The woman sat perched on a stool that looked like a twin to the one in the police department. She looked with mild interest at Annie as she approached. "May I help you?"

"I'm looking for a friend who was visiting in Preacher's Reach," Annie said. "She's fallen out of touch, and I'm worried about her."

The woman's interest turned to concern. "A woman traveling alone?"

"No, she was traveling with a friend," Annie said. She pulled out her wallet and showed the young woman a photo of Alice holding Boots. "This is Alice."

The woman smiled. "I remember her. Really pretty hair. I asked her about the color. I thought I'd like to do mine that color, but she said hers was natural."

"All her life," Annie said. "Could you tell me when you saw her?"

The woman chewed her lip as she thought. "I'm not

sure. Every day is like every other day, ya know? It might have been a week ago, maybe less. I'm sorry."

"Did you talk about anything other than her hair?" Annie asked.

Again, the woman took a moment to think. "She asked me about good places to eat. I like The Fish House and Sandy's Pizza—but stay away from the Pizza Pie Palooza, that stuff is nasty cardboard. The grade school does better pizza."

Annie felt a rush of hope as she quickly wrote down the two more places to check and ask questions. "I really appreciate this," she said. "I've been worried."

"Leslie!"

The sharp voice made both women jump. The cashier looked toward the back of the store at a hawk-nosed, balding man in a long white apron. "I need you back here."

Leslie looked at him in surprise. "I'm with a customer, Walt."

"I need you right now!"

Leslie gave Annie an apologetic shrug. "Coming."

"Thank you," Annie whispered as Leslie headed to the back of the store. Annie wondered if she should wait for the young woman to come back or just go see what her friends had found out. She waited a couple long minutes, but whatever the man had wanted must have been time-consuming as Leslie didn't come back.

Finally, Annie headed outside. She found Mary Beth waiting. "Any luck?" Annie asked.

Mary Beth shook her head. "I guess Alice didn't need anything cleaned. How about you?"

"Actually, yes," Annie said. Before she could say anything else, Ian walked out of the hardware store with a small bag.

"Shopping, Ian?" Annie asked.

"I thought buying something might break the ice."

"Did it work?" Annie asked.

Ian shook his head. "It was weird though. I could have sworn the guy's face changed when I described Jim's limp, but he said he hadn't seen them."

"Well, the lady in the grocery met Alice," Annie said as she held up her small notebook. "And she gave me the name of some restaurants she recommended to Alice. We can ask at these places."

"Fantastic," Mary Beth said. "So, where to now?"

"It's not suppertime yet," Ian said. "I vote we try the boat rental place that the chief mentioned."

"Gets my vote," Mary Beth said.

Annie agreed and they headed quickly back toward the police station parking lot to get Mary Beth's car.

The drive to the boat rental took them down increasingly narrow, bumpy roads. The air was thick with moisture. Annie gazed at the trees as they passed. The trunks were covered with patchy lichen, and the forest floor was dotted with low-growth green plants and clumps of mushrooms.

As Annie watched the passing landscape, she had an idle thought. The woods here were so different from Maine that it was a little like slipping into a fairy tale—or a ghost story with the eerie twisted trees and dripping moss.

The GPS broke into her thoughts as it directed them

to turn just ahead, assuring them that that they would soon "reach their destination."

The small wooden building perched next to the water was well-kept and showed little sign of the dampness and weather it must experience in the swampy area. "I half-expected to see a tumble-down shack and a couple of guys with questionable dental hygiene," Mary Beth said.

"Mary Beth!" Annie scolded. "You watch too many movies."

Ian pulled the SUV into the gravel parking lot, and they piled out. Ian led the group into the small building. An older teenaged girl with long black hair streaked with pink leaned on the tall wooden counter. She stood up when they walked in. "Hi! Welcome to Maynard's. I'm Ellie Maynard."

"Hello," Ian answered. "We were hoping to ask you some questions about a boat you rented."

The girl frowned slightly. "One we rented?"

"A friend of mine rented it," Annie said, pulling out the photo of Alice to show the girl.

The girl looked at the photo, suddenly nervous. She looked up at Annie, then back at the photo. "Well ..." she said.

The sound of footsteps on the wooden porch drew everyone's attention as a man about Annie's age walked in. His face was a road map of fine lines, suggesting a man who'd spent much of his life in the sun. He wore jeans and a faded T-shirt under a fishing vest. "Howdy," he said. "What can I do ya for?"

"They're looking for someone," Ellie said nervously, holding out the photo toward the man.

He took the photo, glanced quickly at it, and handed

it back to Annie. "Yep, I remember her," he said smoothly. "She and a man rented a boat for a day and then dropped it back off after hours."

"Do you know what day this was?" Ian asked.

"Let me check my record book," the man said. He walked behind the counter, and the girl scooted well out of his way. He pulled out a battered spiral-bound book and flipped through the pages. "Here we are." He named the date that would have matched Alice and Jim's first day in Preacher's Reach, the same day that the police chief said they'd come to the police station.

"That's it?" Ian said. "Just the one day?"

The man nodded. "Right, just the one day. We don't get a lot of rentals this time of year, and they were going out to Fuller's Island, which is unusual too. I had to call Chief Harper to clear it since the island is posted land."

"Do you know of any other boat rental they might have used for the rest of their stay?" Ian asked.

The man shook his head. "I got the feeling they were only planning to stay in Preacher's Reach for the one day. The man said they'd only need the boat once."

"Did they mention where they were staying?" Ian asked.

The man shook his head. "Maybe at once of those box motel things along the highway? They get the most over-night traffic since they're so easy to find."

"Did they seem OK?" Annie asked.

"Sure," the man said. "They were laughing and joking."

"We'd like to rent a boat to go out to the island tomorrow," Ian said.

The man shook his head, his face apologetic. "I wish I could. We've got all the boats out of the water for repairs. We do it every year about this time when the tourist trade ends but before the weather turns bad."

"Can you recommend another place we might get a boat?" Ian asked.

"I doubt you'll find one," the man answered. "All the boat rentals pull their boats about this time every year. This area is hard on boats. We do a lot of repair to keep them working during tourist season."

"Well, I appreciate your help," Ian said. Annie heard Mary Beth snort behind her, but Ian acted as if he didn't hear. "Could you tell us your name, just in case, we think of any other questions?"

"I'm Bob Maynard," the man said with a thin smile. "But I'm sure I won't have any other answers for you. I've told you all I know."

"When you went through the boat," Annie said, stepping forward before Ian could tell the man goodbye, "did you happen to see anything my friends might have left behind?"

The man turned his sharp eyes toward her. He paused as if thinking, then shook his head. "No, they returned it really clean. I wish all the tourists did. You know, I expect your friends headed for some area that would be a little more romantic—they seemed like they'd like some place like that."

"You might be right," Ian said smoothly before Annie could refute the man's words. "Thank you for your time."

"Happy to help," the man said. As they turned to leave, the man spoke again, addressing Annie. "You know, ma'am, I expect your friends will contact you soon."

"I hope so," Annie said doubtfully.

When they got outside, Mary Beth opened her mouth to say something, but Ian held up a hand. "In the car," he said softly.

They walked the rest of the way in silence with only the sound of the gravel under their feet and the whining insects accompanying them.

"That guy was lying," Mary Beth said as soon as they were settled in the car with the doors close.

"That's a distinct possibility," Ian said. "Though so far everyone who has confirmed Jim and Alice's presence have either said the same day for seeing them, or were vague enough that it could have been the same day."

"I saw them here more than one day," Annie said. "Alice video-chatted with me for three nights, and every night was from that room at the inn."

Ian nodded. "Probably. Though you're going from memory and your main focus was on Alice. A lot of rooms in places like that look similar."

"Don't tell us you're going over to the dark side here, Ian," Mary Beth said.

Ian shook his head. "I'm just saying that we shouldn't necessarily embrace a conspiracy theory."

Annie sat back in her seat, suddenly very tired, as Ian started the car. She was sure that the room in the chat was the room in the inn—wasn't she? Suddenly, she didn't know what to believe. She looked out at the passing scenery as they drove away. Alice, she thought again, *where are you?*

～ 10 ～

I sat on the sidewalk, letting the discarded mud from the shoes of shoppers mar my clothing beyond repair—or so my mother said later. My attention was caught up in a spider spinning a web in a crack between the shop steps and the wall of the building. The spider was black and thick-bodied. The web looked like a funnel, and I imagined it as a soft, dark tunnel leading insects to their unfortunate end.

—Steven Fuller, 1925

"Well, the last lead we have right now are those two restaurants," Mary Beth said. "And I'm starving. Which one do you think Jim and Alice were most likely to stop at?"

"Normally, I would say The Fish House, especially since this is a coastal spot. But, after a long day?" Annie said. "Maybe pizza. Jim loves pizza, and it would be fast. Hot, fast comfort food has a lot of appeal when you're tired."

"OK, Annie, could you get the GPS to search for local restaurants?" Ian asked. "Maybe Sandy's Pizza will be on the list. Otherwise, we'll have to stop and ask for directions once we get back to a more populated area."

"This does feel like a whole different world, doesn't it?" Mary Beth said. "I'm starting to see how ghost stories could sprout up around here. I wouldn't be surprised to see some kind of monster lurking in the woods."

"I think I'd still find that a surprise," Annie said as she poked her way through the menus on the GPS. "I don't think I'm quite that enchanted by this place." She scanned the list of restaurants in the area. "Both the fish house and the pizza place are here."

"Sounds fine to me. Annie could have it lead us to the pizza place," Ian said. "I'm glad we don't have to stop and ask."

"Stop and ask for directions?" Mary Beth teased. "What would that do to your rep? We all know real men don't ask for directions."

"I actually learned how to ask for directions years ago," Ian said—then he grinned. "My wife teased me into it. She was not a fan of the 'wander around aimlessly until you stumble on your destination' school of driving, and she made that really plain early on."

"Good for her," Mary Beth said.

"Wayne would ask for directions," Annie said. "But I have to admit, he tended to treat it as a last resort. I think he just didn't like stopping, as long as we were moving—even aimlessly, he felt like we were heading *somewhere*."

"Exactly!" Ian said.

"You know that makes no sense," Mary Beth said.

"I could come up with a few things women do that make no sense," Ian said, giving Mary Beth a grin in the rearview mirror.

She rose to the bait. "Like?"

"Buying a million shoes," he said. "Who needs all those shoes? Just buy a good black pair—they go with everything."

"That's just crazy talk," Mary Beth said.

Annie laughed at her two friends. "Can we save the battle of the sexes until after we get some food?"

"I don't know," Ian said. "I think I stand a better chance if you two are faint from hunger."

"Two?" Annie said. "I don't believe I was giving you a hard time."

Ian shot her a quick teasing glance. "Not this time."

Annie shook her head and turned to look back out the window. They had left the swampy forest behind and she found the sunshine cheering. "You know, I don't think I could live in the woods," Annie said.

"Me either," Mary Beth said. "I like noise and places to shop."

"It's not that for me," Annie said. "It's the light. I'm like a plant. I need plenty of sunlight."

"You must find Maine winters challenging," Ian said.

Annie shrugged. "Sometimes. Winters did tend to be brighter in Texas."

"Homesick?" Ian asked, his face suddenly concerned.

"Sometimes," Annie admitted. "Though if I moved back to Brookfield, I'd be homesick for Stony Point. I guess I'm fickle."

"Somehow," Ian said, "I don't believe that for a second."

"If you two are going to flirt," Mary Beth said, "you can drop me at the inn and bring me a salad too."

Annie felt her face heat up. "I was *not* flirting."

"Of course not," Mary Beth said. "But all teasing aside, do we go anywhere near the inn on the way to the pizza place? I'm starting to feel a little worn-out. I wouldn't mind taking a nice long bath myself and having you two bring me a salad."

"Do we go near the inn?" Ian asked. He peered ahead of them on the road. "We're going in that direction right now."

Annie flipped the menu on the GPS to a zoomed-out view. From what she could guess, they would be going close to the inn. "I think so," she said.

"OK. Switch the GPS to take us to the inn," he said.

They made good time to the inn. Though they weren't the only car on the road, they certainly didn't see the kind of traffic they were used to. "I thought the Stony Point roads were quiet," Mary Beth said. "These are almost spooky."

"You can understand why the South has such a rich ghost-story tradition," Annie said.

"Imagine what it must have been like when people didn't have electricity," Ian added. "Travel at night must have been terrifying. Imagine being lost in the dark in a swamp."

"No thanks," Mary Beth said. "I don't need the nightmares. You know New England has plenty of ghost stories too."

"The older stories tend to be different kinds of ghosts than nowadays," Annie said.

"Oh?" Ian glanced at her curiously. "Have you become a ghost-story scholar?"

Annie shook her head. "No. But Alice and I learned a lot through Jim. You know his lighthouse book was full of ghost stories. He told us that those kinds of stories tend to be tied to the natural things people feared in the area."

"Makes sense," Ian said.

As Annie turned back to look out the window again, she thought that her scary story would have to be about not finding her friends, because *that* was the thing that fright-ened her the most.

They dropped Mary Beth off at the inn and drove to Sandy's Pizza. The smell of pizza engulfed them as they walked into the half-empty restaurant, and Annie's stom-ach growled loudly, bringing a chuckle from Ian.

"Sleuthing builds an appetite," Ian said.

Annie was saved from any further teasing by a booming voice from behind the counter. "Just grab a seat wherever you want!"

Annie jumped. A short man with a head full of black curls smiled apologetically. Ian led Annie to a small booth that had a bench seat on only one side. He gestured for her to go first and slid in beside her. Annie was torn between enjoying the brush of Ian's arm against hers and feeling vaguely guilty about it.

A round-faced young man in glasses and a slightly stained white shirt hurried over to their table. "Pizza is pret-ty much all we make," he said, handing them menus. "But it's the best in the South."

"Pizza it is," Ian said. "Though we needed a couple of salads too."

The young man smiled. "We do salad too." He pointed at a box on the menu. "So what can I get you to drink while you choose your pizza toppings?"

"Sweet tea," Annie said. "I so rarely get real Southern sweet tea anymore."

Ian raised his eyebrows. "Is that something special?"

"Well, you have to like *sweet*."

He nodded. "Sweet tea it is."

"Great," the waiter said. "I'll be right back." He dashed off toward the kitchen.

Ian scanned the menu. "Do you know what you want on the pizza?"

"Anything you want is fine," Annie said, and then she paused and wrinkled her nose. "Except anchovies. Anyway, do you think we should show the picture around?"

"Maybe we should eat first," Ian said. "The way the guy at the boat rental acted, I'm not sure I want to eat the food after we stir people up."

"Good point," Annie said. Then she saw the front door open and sat up sharply. Ellie, the young woman from the boat rental, walked in, and Annie saw their waiter rush over to greet her.

"What a surprise," Ian said quietly.

"I thought she knew more than she had a chance to say," Annie said. "I saw her face when the older man was stonewalling us. I don't think she was very happy."

"Billy!" the loud man behind the counter shouted. "Customers now, girlfriend later."

The young waiter's face turned bright scarlet as Ellie slid into a chair at one of the small empty tables. Billy turned and hurried off to the back, coming out moments later with two tall glasses of iced tea. He carried them over and set them in front of Annie and Ian. "Sorry for the wait," he stammered.

"No problem," Ian said. "It wasn't long. We're ready to order."

Billy pulled a pad from his shirt pocket and wrote down Ian's pizza order.

"We'll also want two large salads to go," Ian said. "But please don't bring them until we're done eating."

"Yes, sir." The young man hastily gathered their menus, clearly still embarrassed at being called out by his boss in front of everyone.

"Billy?" Annie said quietly before the waiter could rush off. "Could I show you something?"

"Yes, ma'am?"

Annie slipped Alice's picture out of her pocket and held it close to the table. "Have you seen this woman? We think she might have eaten here with a friend. He has a white beard and a limp?"

Billy's eyes widened as he heard the description and saw the picture. His eyes darted toward the kitchen. He shook his head reluctantly. "No ma'am. I don't remember folks like that."

"Do you think anyone else here might remember them?" Annie asked.

"No ma'am. I'm sure they wouldn't," Billy said. "Folks pass through town so fast, ma'am."

Annie had been lied to more than a few times by people far better at it than the young waiter. He clearly recognized Alice, but someone had told him to pretend he didn't. "Thank you anyway," she said. "I appreciate you taking a look. I'm so worried about my friend."

Billy looked even more guilty at that. He just nodded and rushed off again for the kitchen.

"Do you still think there's no conspiracy here?" Annie asked.

"I'm coming around to the idea," Ian said. Then he

raised an eyebrow. "I thought we were going to wait until *after* we had our food to antagonize the locals."

"I couldn't control myself," Annie admitted.

She looked back toward the table where Ellie sat and found herself looking right into the girl's eyes before Ellie dropped her gaze to the table. Suddenly, Ellie pulled a napkin out of the holder on the table and began scribbling on it. Finally, she hopped up and headed into the kitchen.

Annie shifted her position so she could watch the kitchen door, but Ellie didn't return. Soon Billy came out carrying their pizza. He set it down on the table along with some small plates and napkins. He cut them each a slice and slid it onto their plates.

"I saw Ellie in here earlier," Annie said. "I was hoping to chat with her. Is she still in the kitchen?"

Billy jumped, looking at her wide-eyed. "No. She took her pizza to go."

"Oh, that's too bad," Ian said.

Billy practically ran from their table after that.

"This town is strange," Ian said, turning to watch the swinging kitchen door that Billy had dashed through.

"At least the pizza is good," Annie said. The cheese was gooey with exactly the right amount of stretch. Annie grabbed a napkin to wipe her chin before Ian saw her with a face full of sauce. To her surprise, the napkin underneath the one she'd grabbed had writing on it. She touched Ian's arm, and he turned his head to face her.

Annie tapped the napkin. In block letters it said, "Meet me tonight at midnight on the road to the boat rental—Ellie."

"I guess not everyone in town likes telling lies," Annie said softly.

"That's the thing about conspiracies," Ian said as he picked up his own slice of pizza. "They only work when everyone plays."

~ 11 ~

I was watching the spider and considering whether I should chase an ant into it's lair or merely rip the tunnel apart with a stick when something thumped me hard on the back. It was the end of a cane. As I looked up the cane, I saw an old woman at the other end. This woman was as old as Cook, but even more frightening. Her staring eyes were milky white against her sun-darkened skin. I felt sure that she was a witch. Who else could have such looks and such bony twisted fingers?
—*Steven Fuller, 1925*

When they got back to the inn and delivered the salads, Ian suggested they gather in Stella's room to talk about what they'd learned while the women ate.

"Why does all the best stuff happen when I'm not around?" Mary Beth asked.

"You did get to enjoy being blown off by Bob Maynard," Ian said. "I certainly found that great fun."

Mary Beth did an impressive imitation of Stella's trademark snort of derision. "So, are we going to meet this girl at midnight?"

"I think she might find all of us a little overwhelming," Annie said. She didn't want to leave her friends out, but she didn't want to risk the girl being scared away either.

"I have no interest in wandering through the swamp

at midnight," Stella said. "You can tell me about it in the morning." Then she stopped and frowned slightly. "On second thought, perhaps I should stay up. You could call me when you get back. Then I'll know if anything unfortunate happens, so I can alert the police."

"I don't think we'll have any trouble from this girl," Annie said. "She's just a teenager, and she's scared."

"Unless she's been sent by the man at the boat rental," Stella said. "And she's supposed to lure you to a secluded place. Then the town will pretend no one remembers *us* being here either."

"We'll be careful," Ian said. "And we have you here."

"At the inn that doesn't *remember* Alice and Jim," Stella said.

"I'll stay here with you," Mary Beth said. "We'll put a chair in front of the door and wait to hear from Annie and Ian."

Annie was pretty sure they were being silly and paranoid, but somehow she felt a little better at the thought of Mary Beth and Stella safe behind a blocked door. "We'll call on our way back so you two can get to sleep."

"Thanks," Mary Beth said.

"Maybe we should get a couple of hours rest," Annie said, as she followed Ian out of the room. "Let's meet outside the inn at 11. I also need to remember my sweater."

"Your sweater?" Ian looked at her in surprise. "Are you cold?"

"Not right now, but by midnight, I might be."

"It's good to plan ahead," Ian agreed as he followed her up the stairs.

Annie had purposefully packed a dark-color sweater

just in case they needed to be out late and inconspicuous. She'd learned enough during the various mysteries she'd been through to be prepared. She just hoped she was prepared enough.

*   *   *   *

A little more than two hours later, they were driving slowly along the uneven road toward the boat rental. The darkness was absolute, and the sound of insects in the woods seemed almost deafening.

Since they didn't really know where Ellie was waiting, Ian drove at a crawl. He didn't want to risk running the girl over if she appeared out of the darkness suddenly. They reached the last turn before the boat rental, and Annie caught the flash of a light in the trees. "Ian," she said. "Look!"

Ian pressed the brake, and the car rolled to a stop. The flashlight bobbed through the trees, and Ellie stepped out into the beams of the headlights, shielding her eyes from the brightness. "Well, we know it's Ellie," Annie said.

"Right, please stay in the car until we're sure it's safe," Ian said, his voice low and serious. He cut the headlights, and Ellie became only a dark shadow behind the flashlight beam. Ian got out of the car and stepped toward her. "Ellie?"

The dark shadow bobbed, as if the girl nodded. "Are you alone?" The flashlight turned toward the car windshield.

"Are you?" Ian asked.

Ellie took a step away from him. "Yeah, but I can scream if I have to. My house isn't too far from here."

"No need to scream," Ian said.

Annie swung open her car door and stepped out into the sticky night. "It's just Ian and me, Ellie. It's OK. Did you want to tell us something about our friends?"

The beam of the flashlight swept over Annie. "Uncle Bob is lying, and I don't know why," she said. "Everyone is acting so weird. Your friends rented the boat four times, and they always brought it back before the shop closed, except for the last time."

"The last time when it showed up late at night?" Annie said.

Ellie shook her head. "It never showed up. Uncle Bob took another boat out to the island and towed it back."

"So they could still be on the island?" Annie said.

"Not according to Chief Harper," Ian reminded her. "He said they searched."

"But how hard do you think they looked?" Annie asked. "They thought Alice and Jim had brought the boat back."

"Well, *maybe* they thought it," Ellie said. "I don't know what's going on, but a lot of people are acting weird. Everyone's giving out orders, and no one's telling me anything."

"Like your friend at the pizza parlor?" Annie asked.

"Yeah, his boss told him that if anyone asked, he was supposed to say he didn't remember your friends," Ellie said. "Billy doesn't want to lose his job. There aren't that many jobs to be had around here."

"Do you have any idea who might be behind the misinformation?" Ian asked. "Does it all seem to be your Uncle Bob's idea, or is it coming from somewhere else?"

"I don't think it's Uncle Bob," Ellie said. "I think he's scared."

"You think someone is threatening him?" Annie asked.

Ellie shrugged. "I don't know, but I've never seen my Uncle Bob scared, and he deals with some scary stuff, sometimes, out in the swamp."

"We have to get out to that island," Annie said. "Do you know of anyone who'll rent us a boat?"

Ellie shook her head. "Uncle Bob called a bunch of people after you left. He sent me on errands, but I eavesdropped some first. He was telling folks not to rent to you."

"But you didn't hear him say why?" Ian asked.

"Nothing that made sense. He said that if they rented a boat to you people, it would come back to bite them."

"We have to find a way," Annie said. "If Jim and Alice are on the island, we need to go out there."

"I think we should talk to Chief Harper," Ian said. "When he hears that Jim and Alice didn't return the boat, he'll have to send someone out to do a proper search of the island."

Ellie reached out to clutch at Annie's sleeve. "You can't tell Chief Harper that I told you about the boat. I don't want Uncle Bob to get into trouble."

"Ian, we don't even know if Chief Harper is interested in helping us," Annie said. "It sounds like a lot of people in this town would rather we just gave up and went away."

"Look, I can get you out to the island," Ellie said. "I have a boat. It's not as nice as Uncle Bob's boats, but it'll get you there. It's just that we can't go during the day. I can't let anyone find out that I took you."

"How big is this boat?" Ian asked. "Big enough to take us to the island and bring Jim and Alice back?"

"Big enough," Ellie said. "Though ... it might be better if everyone didn't weigh too much."

"Ellie, is this boat safe?" Ian asked.

"I use it all the time," Ellie said.

Annie noticed that wasn't exactly an answer to Ian's question, but it also sounded like hers was the only boat they were likely to find to take them out to the island. "Maybe you could just tell us where to find the boat," Annie said. "Then you wouldn't get into trouble for helping us."

Ellie shook her head. "The motor is kind of temperamental. And you kinda have to bail sometimes when the pump goes out. I don't want to feel like it's my fault if you two turn up missing too."

"Bailing," Ian muttered. "That's great."

Annie ignored him. "I really appreciate your help. When can you take us to the island? Now?"

"No," Ian said. "If we're going to the island, I want to be sure people know exactly where we are. And I want to bring some emergency equipment. Can you take us tomorrow?"

"Yes," Ellie said. "But if Uncle Bob gets a hint of this, I won't be able to help you anymore."

"Then we better learn what we need to know in the first trip," Ian said.

"Let me have your cell number," Ellie said. "I'll call you as soon as I can get away."

They exchanged numbers, and Ellie quickly headed into the woods. They saw the bobbing light of her flashlight for a while, and then nothing. Ian and Annie got back in the SUV, and Ian turned around in the bend of the road in silence.

Once they were on sure roads back to the inn, Ian called Mary Beth and Stella to let them know they were on their way back. He then took a deep breath and said, "I don't like this. It feels too dangerous."

"Ellie has helped us more than anyone else in town," Annie said. "If Jim and Alice are on the island, I'm willing to take the risk."

"But what happens if Ellie's boat sinks halfway to the island?" Ian asked.

"The island is barely a half mile from the mainland," Annie said. "I can swim that far—can't you?"

"In the dark?" Ian said. "With who knows what in the water? Maybe. But do you think Stella can?"

Annie shook her head. "No, but we shouldn't all go anyway. Someone should stay on this side and call for help if we need it."

"I need to think about this," Ian said.

"I don't," Annie answered. "Jim and Alice might be on that island. And I'm going out there. If you want to stay on shore and be part of the safety line, I'm fine with that."

"That's the kind of wild idea that drives me crazy," Ian said, glaring out at the darkness in front of them as he drove. "You take a lot of risks with your own safety. I don't like this. I don't want you hurt."

"And I don't want to *be* hurt," Annie said. "But I can't just wait for Alice to turn up. I have to look for her."

Ian nodded but didn't say anything else, and they finished the drive to the inn in silence.

"I'm comfortable being your mainland safety net," Stella said. "I have no interest in swimming when the boat sinks."

"I'll risk a swim," Mary Beth said. "I really want to see the island. And if Jim and Alice are stuck somewhere, you might need all the hands you can get."

"Especially if you're searching in the middle of the night," Stella said.

Ian crossed his arms over his chest and looked around the room. "I still reserve the right to veto this plan when I see the boat," he said.

Mary Beth stood up and gave him a pat on the arm as she headed for the door. "You can certainly try vetoing, Mr. Mayor. Now, I'm heading up to bed. If we're having an adventure tomorrow, I need my sleep."

"I need mine also," Stella said. "I'll see you all tomorrow."

Ian frowned, but he allowed Stella to herd them out of the room. "This discussion isn't over," he told Annie quietly as they walked up the stairs toward their rooms.

"Sleep well," Annie said sweetly.

Annie was surprised to discover that she did sleep well and woke excited to finally have a lead about Alice and Jim. The group gathered in the charming breakfast room of the inn. Sunday brunch proved to be very popular, as Mrs. Ayers had warned. As they ate the delicious food, Annie felt curious eyes turned their way from all over the room.

"We're certainly popular," Mary Beth said as she cut her slice of country ham and took a bite. "Oh, yum. I thought the eggs were lovely, but this ham is amazing."

"So are the crepes," Stella said; then she glanced around the room. "One would think food this good would have the attention of everyone in the room. Instead, it seems we do."

"From what we've heard," Ian said as he cut into a fluffy

pancake, "we're the talk of the town."

"But we are definitely not the people the town wants to talk to," Annie said. She scanned the room but wasn't able to catch anyone's eye. As soon as anyone saw her looking, they suddenly became very focused on the plates in front of them.

"So what's on for the daylight hours?" Mary Beth asked quietly.

"I think we should keep asking questions," Annie said. "We don't want anyone to think we're starting to get any answers."

"Where do you want to start asking?" Stella asked.

"I believe we should visit the historical society," Annie said. "We know Jim spoke to someone there—at least on the phone."

"That sounds reasonable," Ian told her. "Shall we all descend on them?"

"Maybe not all of us," Annie said. "I wonder if we should also ask at other restaurants and inns, just to look properly clueless."

"How about we split up?" Mary Beth said. "I could drop you and Ian at the historical society, and then Stella and I could check out some of the local restaurants and inns. I have a photo of Alice from a Hook and Needle Club meeting that I can show around. You could call me when you're done with the historical society, and I'll pick you up."

"We should probably ask at the newspaper office too," Annie said. "I saw that it was right next to the historical society."

"That sounds reasonable," Stella said.

With the plan in place, they focused on the meal for the rest of the time, chatting about more normal things. Annie let the conversation wash over her, but found she simply couldn't lose herself in normal chatter. Within a matter of hours, she might finally have some answers about Jim and Alice.

She jumped when she felt a warm hand cover hers. "Did you sleep last night?" Ian asked quietly.

"Better than I expected," Annie admitted. "Though I was a little wired at first. I am so happy that we're making some headway. I'm just having trouble waiting."

"Don't think of it as waiting," Ian said. "We may learn some important things today, even before nightfall."

"Of course," Annie said, smiling. Then she looked around at her friends and noticed everyone had finished eating. Her own plate had more food moved around than eaten, but she had no interest in eating more. "Shall we get started?" she asked.

The drive to the historical society reminded them again of just how beaten down the small town looked. They passed several buildings that had once housed stores of one sort or another, but now the shops had broken windows, and weeds grew from the deep cracks in the parking lots.

Mary Beth pulled onto the cracked pavement that surrounded the *Preacher's Reach News* office. "Since it's Sunday, I'll wait while you see if the historical society or newspapaer office are even open."

"Good idea," Ian said. He and Annie climbed out of the SUV and hurried across the pavement toward the historical society building. Annie could feel the baking heat right through the soles of her shoes.

The metal and glass door of the historical society had no hours posted, but the door opened easily when Annie pulled on it. She stepped into the cool interior. Ian waved toward Mary Beth's SUV before following Annie inside.

The interior was dimly lit and mostly one large room with only a few windows high on the walls. Cheap bookcases, stuffed with books and boxes, lined the wall space. A few battered tables were piled with more books and stacks of papers. "Anyone here?" Annie called.

A door opened near the far corner and a woman in a neat suit walked out. "I'm sorry," she said. "I didn't know anyone was here. I really should get a bell for the door."

"You probably don't get a lot of Sunday visitors," Ian said.

"Not so many," the woman agreed. "How can I help you? Are you looking for the local cemeteries? I do have some maps."

"Actually, we're not interested in cemeteries," Annie said.

"Really?" the woman seemed surprised. "Most tourists who come in are asking about the old cemeteries—especially slave cemeteries. It was quite 'the thing' for a while."

"Oh," Annie said. "Do you have a lot of slave cemeteries?"

"Not really," the woman said. "A few small ones." Then she smiled. "Forgive me my manners. I'm Beatrice Harlow."

"My name is Annie Dawson, and this is my friend Ian Butler," Annie said. "We're actually interested in Fuller's Island."

"Really?" the woman smiled indulgently. "Just the island or are you interested in other haunted areas as well. I have maps … ."

"Do you have many haunted areas?" Ian asked.

"Well, one of the slave cemeteries is said to be quite active," the woman said. "And the Bonneau's Plantation House. It's an inn now with a ridiculous name. Preacher's Rest they call it. The owners don't really like ghost hunting—well, Mrs. Ayers doesn't. Her brother is much more open to it, but he's so rarely around. At any rate, with Mrs. Ayers not being appreciative of seekers of the spirit realm, any investigation must be done discreetly."

"What about you?" Ian asked. "Are you open to it?"

"I like to think of myself as open-minded," Mrs. Harlow said.

"Perhaps you met some friends of ours," Annie said. "They're both very open-minded, and they were especially interested in Fuller's Island."

The old woman wrinkled her nose. "It wasn't that young couple from the Adventurer's Club? They were *not* open-minded ... not really. At least the young man wasn't. I can sense these things. I think they just liked getting attention. He kept talking about going 'viral,' whatever that means."

"Those aren't the people we're looking for, but I think I saw a video that the young couple made," Annie said. "Did they visit Fuller's Island recently?"

The old woman nodded. "In the late summer."

"Are they the last people who showed an interest in the island?" Ian asked.

"No," the woman said. "There was that nice couple in love. The man said he was a photographer. They were very polite, and I believe they are both very open to extraordinary experiences. I could sense it."

Annie quickly pulled the photo of Alice from her pocket. "Was this the woman?"

"Oh yes," the woman said, smiling and nodding. "Such a pretty girl, and I could tell her beau doted on her."

Annie smiled. Alice should hear herself called a girl. "Yes, he does. What did you tell them about the island?"

"Well, there's the legend, of course," the woman said. "But I went out to the island many times when I was young. It was the thing for teenagers to do after the sanitarium closed. I mostly saw kudzu, Spanish moss, and mud. I'm very sensitive, so if there were ghosts, I think I would know."

"I'm sure you would," Ian said. "But would you be willing to tell us the legend anyway?"

Mrs. Harlow beamed at him. "Certainly, I don't mind. Shall we sit? My hips and back do get tired of standing after a while."

"Of course," Ian quickly pulled up a chair for the woman, and then he unloaded books from a couple of other chairs for himself and Annie.

"It really all started when Matthew Steven Fuller offended one of the mainland women, Maggie Cantrell. "She was a witch for sure, that one," Mrs. Harlow said. "She cursed the Fullers and their island—called the hounds of hell down on the family. Said as long as Fullers lived on the island, the hounds would hunt."

"And they did?" Ian said when the woman paused.

"So the story goes," Mrs. Harlow said. "Three servants were injured by the hounds as well as some mainland people who may have been poaching on the land. Then Mr. Fuller himself was attacked, and he died from the injuries. His family all gathered for the funeral, but they left altogether soon after. Everyone here 'bouts thought they'd never be back, but then the old man's great-grand-son moved to the island after the war and set up his sanitarium for the wealthy."

"How did the local people feel about that?" Ian asked.

"Well, they weren't happy," Mrs. Harlow said. "Him tempting the curse like that. I have to say he tried. He kept his family there even after his patients started leaving him—all scared away by the hounds."

"Were there more attacks?" Ian said.

"No—except for the one on the doctor himself," Mrs. Harlow said. "That's when the family moved to the mainland. They lived just outside Preacher's Reach for a while, and his daughter even married a local boy. I can tell you that her Mama didn't like that much. Anyway, when the daughter moved away with her new husband, the Fullers became hermits. No one ever saw them in town."

"Maybe they did their shopping somewhere else?" Annie said.

Mrs. Harlow shrugged. "Maybe. At any rate, no one has reported any ghostly happenings on the island since then."

"Except for the young couple that you mentioned," Annie said. "They put a video on their website that certainly made it seem like they were chased by dogs."

The woman shook her head. "I wouldn't believe a speck of it. I tell you, I was on the island about thirty years ago.

There's not a ghost there. I'd stake my reputation on it."

Then she smiled and lowered her voice. "Though I have begun to suspect the island has had visitations."

"Visitations?" Annie echoed. "From who?"

The old woman pointed upwards.

"From God?" Ian asked, confused.

She shook her head. "From aliens. People have been reporting lights. And alien visitations are quite common along the coast."

"Oh," Annie said, not sure what to say.

Mrs. Harlow straightened in her chair and smiled. "But if it's ghosts you're interested in, you really should check out that inn. Take a little walk out beyond the out buildings. All that overgrown field? There are graves there, and they're restless."

"Thank you," Ian said. "We'll check that out."

Mrs. Harlow smiled. "Good. I used to walk out there to commune with the spirits, but Mrs. Ayers didn't like that. She said it was bad for business. What do the spirits care about business?"

"Probably not much," Ian said agreeably.

"You're right, not much," the old woman said.

"Mrs. Harlow," Annie asked, "did my friends give you any idea of what they planned to do while in Preacher's Reach?"

"No, they said they wanted to go out to the island," Mrs. Harlow said. "I told them to check with Bob Maynard for a boat. I babysat that boy when he was in diapers. I like to send him a speck of business when I can."

"Has Bob Maynard ever been in any trouble?" Ian asked.

"No, not really," Mrs. Harlow said. "Though I still believe

he was part of the miscreant group that tossed toilet paper into my trees one Halloween. Made a horrible mess when it rained. And he was quite sweet on my daughter at one time, but nothing seemed to come of *that*. It may be just as well, considering the toilet paper incident."

"Sounds terrible," Annie said.

"If I'd gotten outside a bit faster, I'd have taken a switch to those boys," Mrs. Harlow said. "But they only did it the one time."

"That's good," Annie said.

"Overall though, he's a good boy," Mrs. Harlow said. "But you know how boys are, so easily led astray."

"Mrs. Harlow," Ian said, "we thought we might ask at the newspaper office. Do you know if anyone will be in there today?"

The old woman nodded, smiling. "My Nora should be there, getting the Monday paper ready."

"Your Nora?" Ian echoed.

"Yes, my daughter," the old woman said. "She went off to North Carolina to learn all about being a newspaper publisher, and then she came back here and started the paper back up. She's even won a couple awards."

"You must be very proud of her," Annie said.

"I am," Mrs. Harlow said; then she sighed. "Now if she had just met a nice young man and had given me some grandchildren. But I guess you can't have everything."

"I guess not," Annie said. "I think we're going to stop and speak to Nora for a few minutes. Do you think she'll have time?"

"Oh sure," Mrs. Harlow said. "My Nora has manners,

not like some I could name. She'll be happy to see you."
The old woman stood stiffly and pushed some pamphlets
into Annie's hand. "Here are the maps I told you about.
You should visit some of the places in the moonlight." She
leaned close. "It's very romantic."

Ian flashed her a smile. "I'll look forward to it."

The old woman's back was bent, but she leaned over still further until her face loomed close to mine. Her breath smelled like stale cigarettes and death. "Do you think you're safe, boy?" she asked me. "Do you think the devil's hounds cannot find such a little, little boy?" The old woman tapped her nose then. "They don't need to see you. They smell you. Nothing smells quite like a Fuller." I tried to scream for my mother, but my throat felt closed, and I could barely breathe. The old witch ran bent fingers through my hair and laughed, pointing at my lap. To my shame, I had wet myself from fear.

—Steven Fuller, 1925

The walk back across the broken pavement seemed even hotter than before. It was warm for an October day. "I do believe I've lost my thin Texas blood," Annie said. "This heat is brutal."

"I am going to appreciate autumn when we get home," Ian agreed as they reached the door to the newspaper office. As Mrs. Harlow had suggested, the door opened easily.

The interior of the cinder-block building felt like an oven. They found a woman hunched over a desk, frowning into a bulky computer monitor. The woman looked to be somewhere in her early forties with dark blond curls pulled back into a bushy ponytail. The woman looked up as they came in. "Can I help you?"

"Nora Harlow?" Ian asked.

"That's me," she said. "Something I can do for you?"

"I hope so," Annie said. "We're looking for some friends and thought they might have stopped here when they were in town." Annie held out the photo of Alice.

The woman took the photo, mopping her forehead with her arm as she looked at it. "I remember her. Alice—her name is Alice, right?"

Annie smiled. "Right. And she would have been with Jim Parker."

Nora nodded. "He had a fine camera with him. I wish I could afford equipment like that for the newspaper. He said he was going to take some photos out on Fuller's Island."

"Yes, and we know they made it out there," Annie said. "But they've disappeared."

"Disappeared?" The woman's eyes widened. "Around here?"

Annie nodded. "She told me they were going out to the island for some twilight photography, and I never heard from them again."

"You don't think they could have just finished up and moved on?" Nora asked.

"Alice knows Annie worries," Ian said. "She wouldn't have stayed out of touch this long."

"Plus, we know they took a boat out to the island and never brought it back," Annie said.

"Have you talked to Chief Harper?"

"Yes, and he sent an officer out to the island but didn't find anything," Ian said.

Nora frowned. "Did he say which officer?"

"Leroy."

Nora shook her head. "Leroy couldn't find his, um, head with both hands." She stopped and sat back in her chair. She looked pensive for a moment, and then added, "Chief Harper is a good guy, but he's not fond of tourists. A lot of our local guys are like that."

"I'm not much interested in Chief Harper's prejudices," Ian said. "We just want to find our friends."

"I don't like hearing that they disappeared on the island," Nora said. "I've been out there—not in recent years—but back when I was a teenager. The buildings are falling down. It's not a safe place. I told your friends that, and if they're missing ... ."

"You think they could be hurt," Annie said.

"They could be," Nora agreed. "You should get Bob Maynard to send a boat out and look around. I know he takes tourists out there. The fishing around the island is fantastic."

"Bob Maynard didn't seem overly interested in helping us," Annie said. She longed to tell Nora what Ellie had told them, but didn't want to get the girl in trouble. "A lot of people around here don't seem interested in helping us."

"Let me see what I can do," Nora said. She fished in her pockets until she came up with a cellphone, and then punched in a number. "Hi, it's Nora. I'm trying to find out what happened to a couple of tourists who wanted to take pictures on Fuller's Island. Can you take me out there?"

Annie held her breath, waiting to hear what came next.

"All of them? You have all of your boats out of the water? Come on, Bob, this is Nora you're talking to. No, I'm not. No. Look, rent me a rowboat then. Why are you being such a jerk?" At that the call ended, and the look on Nora's face made it clear that Bob had hung up on her. She looked up at Ian and Annie. "Just what hornet's nest have y'all been kicking?"

"We're just looking for our friends," Ian told her.

Nora stood up and smiled. "And suddenly, I want to do a little looking of my own."

"Can you get us out to the island?" Ian asked.

"Not with Bob's help, but he's not the only boat in the sea," she said. "Look, give me a little time and let me see what I can turn up. Can I get your phone numbers? I'll call you and tell you what I've found."

Annie smiled and quickly scrawled her number on the torn bit of paper Nora had given her. "I really appreciate this," she said. "We've run into so many stone walls."

"You kick a wall long enough," Nora said, "and it crumbles. And I *really* want to see what's behind this one."

"Bob Maynard isn't the only person who is keeping secrets," Ian said. "Alice and Jim stayed at the Preacher's Rest Inn, but when our own police chief called around, no one would admit to renting to them. And we believe they ate at Sandy's Pizza, but we got very nervous denials there too."

"What exactly were your friends here to do?" Nora said. "They told me they just wanted to take pictures of the old buildings. I don't see how that could produce this kind of reaction. We get tourists tromping around all the time. The ghost busters alone are like mosquitoes around here."

"That's really what they came to do," Annie said. "Take pictures."

"No secret investigative journalism stuff?" Nora asked.

"No."

Nora crossed her arms over her chest and shook her head. "This doesn't make any sense. Well, I'm a newspaperwoman—when I find a good hornet's nest, I gotta poke it. I'll let you know what I find out."

"Just don't get hurt," Annie said.

After a few more assurances of calls and carefulness, Ian and Annie walked back outside. Ian pulled out his phone and called Mary Beth as they walked across the paved lot to a small patch of scrubby grass that circled a swamp maple nearby. The shade of the tree offered some welcome cover from the sun.

Annie leaned against the smooth bark of the tree. "Well, it's good to find someone else who thinks this is all very weird."

"I have to admit, I'd hoped Nora could find us a boat," Ian said. "Something a little more seaworthy. I'm still not excited about our night excursion."

"She still might," Annie said. "Local people might not be as quick to shut her out."

"It sounded like Bob Maynard was," Ian said. "Maybe we should take her with us to the island tonight."

"I don't think we should without asking Ellie," Annie said. "The girl was scared. I don't want to put her in any danger."

"If she regularly takes a boat that she admits to bailing around these shores at night," Ian said, "I'm not sure *we're* the ones putting her in danger."

Annie smiled. "Where's your sense of adventure?" she teased.

Ian crooked an eyebrow, but before he could say anything, they heard the quick toot of a car horn. They turned toward the parking lot to see Mary Beth's SUV pull up. Annie was thrilled to slip into the cool interior of the car. It was almost like jumping into a pool after being out in the roasting sun.

"I hope you two did better than us. We ran into so many brick walls," Mary Beth complained, "that I'm surprised my nose isn't flat."

"We had a little better luck," Annie said. Then she launched into a description of their conversations with both Mrs. Harlow and Nora.

"Nice to find someone else on our side," Mary Beth said when Annie finished.

"Except she seems to be getting the same kinds of answers we did," Stella added.

"So far," Ian agreed. "But she's going to keep digging, and she knows these people."

"It sounds to me like we're basically done for the day," Stella said. "Until you hear from Ellie, I vote for a nice relaxing afternoon at the inn."

"I wouldn't be opposed to that," Mary Beth said. "I could spend a few hours crocheting. I've been so busy I haven't finished even one piece for the tornado victims gift drive. After I talked everyone into taking part in the drive, it won't look good if I don't have anything myself."

"OK," Ian agreed. "I brought along a book to read." Then he glanced at Annie with a smile. "Unless, that is, you want to wander with me in the field behind the inn and commune with the spirits?"

"Not in this heat," Annie said. "Though I wouldn't mind communing with a tall sweet tea."

When they reached the inn, they found that Mrs. Ayers had made pitchers of sweet iced tea. Apparently the Sunday "brunch" crowd lasted most of the day, as a number of people had settled into the wicker chairs on the long porches and sipped tea.

Stella and Mary Beth headed for their rooms to collect needlework projects, while Annie and Ian found chairs on the porch and gratefully accepted glasses of ice-cold tea. Ian wrinkled his nose at the first sip. "It still seems a little sweet to me," he said.

"The sugar helps you feel less drained by the heat," Annie said.

"Really?"

Annie laughed. "No, probably not, but it sounds good."

Ian leaned back in his chair and chuckled. He closed his eyes and rubbed the cold, damp glass against his brow. "Now that helps with the heat."

Annie gazed across the street from the inn, and suddenly realized she was looking at a cemetery. "Ian," she said. "Didn't Mrs. Harlow say the cemetery was behind the inn?"

"The one across the street was for white folks," a woman beside them said. "The one out back was for slaves."

Annie turned in her seat to face a tiny dark-skinned lady who wore a white hat perched on top of her close-cropped gray curls. "Oh," Annie said.

The lady smiled at her. "All sorts of folks are buried in that cemetery *now*," she said, nodding toward the street. "The folks in the old graves would be right disgruntled to know who they're sharing ground with these days."

"Do you think so?" Annie said, musing. "I would like to think people get over themselves after death."

The other woman chuckled. "Could be. Though I've found folks can hold onto things for a long, long time. Certainly they can down here. You have a bit of the South in your voice, but you're not from around here. Texas?"

"Yes," Annie said, smiling. "A little town called Brookfield. Though I live in Maine now."

The other woman nodded. "I thought your friend sounded like a Yankee. So what brings y'all down here?"

"We're actually looking for friends who came here and disappeared," Annie said.

"Oh my, that sounds ominous. You mean disappeared from Preacher's Reach?"

"Or from Fuller's Island," Annie said.

"That island can be dangerous," the other woman said. "Nasty swamps and crumbling buildings."

"And curses?" Annie asked.

The woman snorted. "I hope you don't put any stock in such foolishness."

"No, but I didn't think grown people could just disappear either."

"You're right there," the woman said. "If someone disappears, the answer isn't in any demon dog curse."

"So you *do* know the story," Annie said.

The other woman leaned back in her chair and closed

her eyes. "My family has lived 'round here for a long time. I've heard all the stories."

"Do you know why people would cover up a disappearance?" Annie asked.

"It's been my experience that most folks do bad things for one of two reasons," the woman said, her eyes still closed. "Money or fear. You just gotta find out which one is happening here."

"Do you know which?" Annie asked.

"No, ma'am," the woman said. "I do not, but I surely haven't seen much money in Preacher's Reach in a long time. If someone's found a way to get some, they're likely doing something God would frown on fiercely."

Annie leaned back in her own chair again, gazing across the street but not really seeing anything. Money or fear, was one at work in Preacher's Reach? Or were both?

The long days of worry finally caught up with Annie as the drowsy afternoon heat lay on her, and she fell asleep. She dreamed she was wandering through a strange mazelike version of Grey Gables looking for Alice. She kept calling her friend's name and hearing a faint call in return, but no matter how many halls Annie walked down and how many stairs she climbed, she couldn't seem to get any closer to Alice.

She awoke with a start when Ian laid his hand on her arm. He was holding his cellphone to his ear. "*Ellie,*" he mouthed.

Annie turned to glance at the chair on the other side of her. The tiny woman in the white hat was gone. In fact, the porch was empty except for Ian and Annie. Annie noticed the sun was low in the sky and realized she must have napped for a couple of hours.

"I don't know how much we'll be able to find in the pitch dark," Ian said. "I hate to run the risk for nothing."

He seemed to listen for a long time, and Annie felt almost itchy as she waited to learn what Ellie had said. Finally Ian said, "Is that safe?"

More waiting. Annie resisted the urge to tug on his arm and demand to know what Ellie was saying. All she'd manage to do then would be to make sure neither of them heard the girl. "OK," Ian said sharply. "We'll be there."

As he slipped his phone back in his pocket, he said, "We should go find Stella and Mary Beth. No point going through this more than once."

Annie was wild to know what Ellie had said, but she nodded and followed Ian into the inn. Next time, she decided, she'd be sure to give out just her number so she didn't have to suffer so much from curiosity.

They found Mary Beth and Stella both in a small sitting room across the foyer from the dining room. Their friends looked up at them curiously. "Did you get the call?" Mary Beth asked.

Ian nodded as he walked over to sit on the chair closest to Mary Beth and Stella. Annie sat on an ottoman beside him and tried not to fidget. "Ellie will meet us at the same place and same time as last night," he said.

"You're going to try to find Alice and Jim in a maze of broken buildings and swamp after midnight?" Stella asked incredulously.

Ian shook his head. "We'll be doing a little camping out.

Ellie will hide her boat from prying eyes, and we'll wait for dawn. Then we'll start searching."

"That makes a little more sense," Stella said. "But it still sounds unpleasant."

"It's search and rescue," Mary Beth said. "Not a spa day."

"*Maybe* it's search and rescue," Stella said. "And maybe it's just search ... and be miserable."

Annie held up a hand. "It does sound unpleasant, but we need to do it. And you'll be safe and dry right here, Stella."

"I think it would be wise for those of us who are going on this adventure to catch a nap if possible," Ian said. "It's going to be a long night."

The group made plans for meeting up, and then each of them drifted off to their rooms to rest. Annie doubted she would be able to sleep, especially after her nap on the porch, but she soon discovered she was wrong. The poor sleep from days of worry had caught up with her in a big way, and she nodded off immediately.

She woke with a start in her dark room well ahead of the alarm. She decided to take a shower and see if she could wash away some of the cobwebs. Over the sound of the hot water she heard her phone. Annie shut off the water and reached out to snag the phone from the bathroom sink where she'd left it.

"Annie?" a woman's voice said tentatively. "This is Nora Harlow. I'm sorry to call so late. I know it's rude."

"That's not a problem," Annie said as she stepped out of the shower and wrapped one of the inn's thick towels around herself. "Did you find out anything about Jim and Alice?"

"I certainly found out that no one wants to talk about

them," Nora said. "People are acting scared—people who don't normally scare all that easily."

Annie was tempted to tell her that Ellie had said virtually the same thing. "Do you have any idea what's scaring them?"

"No, and that's what's so weird," Nora said. "It's like some kind of conspiracy was growing in my backyard, and I didn't notice it. That's not an easy thing for a newspaper-woman to swallow."

"Do you think it could have anything to do with drugs?" Annie asked tentatively. "Like smuggling?"

"No. Most of these people wouldn't get anywhere near drugs," Nora said. "And our coast here is not very good for smuggling by boat or air. Whatever is going on, I don't think it's drugs."

"Anyway, I'm still looking for someone to take me out to the island," Nora said. "Or at least tell me what's going on. I have some people who owe me more than lies. I'll try some face-to-face time tomorrow and see what I can manage. Then I'll let you know."

Again Annie felt the urge to tell Nora about Ellie's boat, but she resisted. For tonight, she would keep the teenager's secret. After the call, Annie dressed quickly in a pair of dark jeans, a dark T-shirt and the dark sweater she'd taken along before. Then she sat cross-legged on the bed and pulled her notebook from her purse. She flipped to an empty page and wrote "What we know" across the top.

What did they know? They knew Jim and Alice had made it to Preacher's Reach. Alice had stayed at the Preacher's Rest Inn—in the room Stella now had. Suddenly Annie had a thought; she flipped to a second page and wrote: "What happened to Alice and Jim's luggage?"

Logically, the luggage might be somewhere at the inn, but it definitely wasn't in Stella's room. So where was it? And where was Jim's car? Annie tapped the question page, and then she flipped back. What else did they know?

She wrote down: "Alice and Jim rented a boat from Bob Maynard." Annie stared at the page. That meant both Mrs. Ayers and Bob Maynard were somehow involved. She flipped to a third page and began listing those who were definitely involved somehow, adding in the owner of Sandy's Pizza.

Her next note read: "Alice and Jim made it out to the island." In fact, they knew Alice and Jim had been on the island more than once without seeing anything mysterious. Alice would have mentioned it if they had. Annie's conversations with Alice had been very normal right up until they disappeared, so if something illegal was happening on the island, it either wasn't easy to spot or didn't happen very often.

"They were going back to explore the island early in the evening." Annie underlined that one twice. It wasn't until Alice and Jim went out to the island at twilight that they disappeared. Did that make a difference? Was there something hidden that could only be found after dark? Or had someone waited until it was dark to do something to Alice and Jim?

Annie sighed and flipped her notebook closed. This wasn't really making her feel better. Still, she decided to mention the luggage and car questions to Ian, Stella, and Mary Beth. Annie glanced at the clock—it was time to rendezvous with her friends.

She slipped quietly out of her room and found Ian waiting in the hall. He held a finger to his lips and then stepped close to her so that he could whisper in her ear. His warm breath on her neck made her shiver. "Do you have a flashlight?" he asked.

Annie nodded and patted her purse. Ian smiled back as he took Annie's hand and started down the hall toward the stairs. Annie followed, looking down at her hand in surprise. She was hardly going to get lost in the dim light of the hall. She didn't need Ian to lead her by the hand. Though—if she were honest—she'd have to admit that it felt very nice.

They crept quietly down the stairs and spotted Stella and Mary Beth near the front door. Annie looked at Stella in surprise as she'd expected her friend to sleep through their leaving since she wasn't coming. They stepped out onto the front porch together.

"Nice of you to see us off," Ian said to Stella.

"I wanted to see if you had any last-minute 'jobs' for me," Stella said. "Something I can do while you're poking around the swamps."

"Well," Annie said, "I did realize that Jim and Alice's luggage might be around here somewhere. And we don't know what happened to Jim's car."

Stella frowned. "I can't imagine they have the car hidden here, but I could look around for the luggage a little."

"Just be careful," Ian said sternly.

Annie told her friends quickly about the call from Nora. "She might be able to help with ideas about where Jim's car might be hidden," she said. "I just wish I'd thought of it while I was talking to her."

"Who knows?" Mary Beth said. "We might find Jim and Alice tonight. Then all of us together can go looking for Jim's car."

Annie appreciated the optimism, even if she had trouble sharing it. With a few more commands to "be careful," they finally headed out to the SUV while Stella slipped back into the inn. Annie looked worriedly after Stella. The old woman was more than formidable, but she was still by herself. It certainly wouldn't be any harder to make *her* disappear than it was Alice and Jim. Ian gently tugged on Annie's hand, and she followed him reluctantly.

They reached the car, and Mary Beth pulled open the door. She sighed, and shut it again. "I can't do it. I can't leave Stella here to poke around alone. I'd worry about her the whole time. I'm going to stay here. You two can handle the island adventure on your own—OK?"

Annie let out of whoosh of relieved breath. "I'm so glad you said that. I was going to worry myself sick about Stella."

"Thanks, Mary Beth," Ian said. "But you be careful too."

"I will." Mary Beth gave them each a quick hug before hurrying back to the inn.

The drive to meet Ellie passed quickly with neither Annie nor Ian having much to say. Since they knew exactly where the girl would be on the road, Ian didn't have to creep along. When they finally slowed to a stop, Annie and Ian both got out of the car and waited for the flash of Ellie's light.

Ellie spoke in an urgent whisper when she came out of the woods. "You need to back up some. There's a road down to a little dock. No one uses it anymore because it was wrecked so bad in the last hurricane. There's a kind of boathouse where you can hide your car."

"Hop in—you can show me," Ian said.

Annie climbed into the back as Ellie hopped into the front passenger seat and pointed out the road for Ian. Even with the girl pointing directly at it, Annie had trouble finding any break in the brush. As they rolled slowly down the overgrown road, tree branches slapped at the SUV, and the car's tires crawled over the uneven ground with bumps and groans.

Finally Ellie directed them behind a tumbledown building. "No one really comes down here," Ellie said. "But it's still better if you're kinda hidden."

They all piled out of the car and followed Ellie to the boat. Even in the soft light of the full moon, Annie could tell the small boat was old and tired. The boat appeared to be made of wood, judging by splintered edges. The tiny wheelhouse almost looked homemade, like a ragged potting shed mounted in the middle of the boat. Ian took one look at it and said, "Forget it, Annie. You're not getting in that thing."

"It's better than it looks," Ellie said loyally, patting her poor boat's rail. "And it's the only boat willing to go out to Fuller's Island."

"Then it's the one I'm riding in," Annie said, stepping down from the half-rotted dock to the worn deck. "You can go help Mary Beth and Stella find luggage. Maybe you can find Jim's car too."

"Annie Dawson," Ian said, his voice almost a growl. "Get out of that boat."

"No." She crossed her arms over her chest and glared at him.

Ellie looked from one to the other and began fiddling with the lines that held the boat to the dock.

"Don't make me pick you up and haul you out of there," Ian said. "That boat is one stiff breeze away from a swim."

"It's the only boat available," Annie said. "And Ellie trusts it. Plus, in case you haven't noticed, you're not my father."

Ian huffed and ran a hand through his short hair. "I'm not trying to be your *father*."

"Then be my *friend*," Annie said, holding out a hand to him. "Come and help me find Alice and Jim."

Ian shot a glance at Ellie. "Do you have life jackets?"

"Sure," Ellie said. She hopped into the boat and walked into the wheelhouse. She tossed out two of the worst-looking life jackets Annie had ever seen. They were covered with dark splotches and stank of mildew.

"I suspect I might prefer drowning," Annie said as she looked down at them.

Ian stepped down into the boat and picked up one of the vests. The stench even wrinkled his nose. Still he shrugged into it and held out the other for Annie. "You wear it, or we get out."

Annie sighed and pulled on the jacket, trying to breath shallowly through her mouth. It didn't help much. The stink seemed to coat her tongue. At least the island wasn't far.

Ellie cast off the lines and disappeared into the wheelhouse again. She passed through to the other side and squatted to start an ancient boat motor. Apparently the shed in the middle of the boat was less wheelhouse and more storage shed.

Ellie fiddled with the motor for so long that it looked like Ian might get his wish—without a working motor, they would have a very long trip. Finally the motor coughed and sputtered before settling into a fairly regular—if tentative—rumble.

Ian pulled Annie down beside him to squat on the deck of the boat. "I think we should keep our weight low," he said.

"Fine with me," Annie said as cheerfully as she could, considering her mouth felt like she'd been licking slime mold.

They made the short trip to the island in relative silence, with the only conversation coming from Ellie's coaxing of her engine and Ian's occasional dark muttering. They followed the rocky coast of the island for a while until a dark gap suddenly appeared. "We'll tie up in here," Ellie called as she cut the motor. "No one can see us from the mainland in here."

She hopped over the side of the boat into the shallow water and clambered quickly up the sandy shore. She wrapped a tie rope around the nearest tree and used the leverage to pull the boat closer before tying off.

Ian hopped over the side with a soft splash. He held his arms up to Annie. "It's not far," he said. "I can help you hop over. That way you can stay out of the water."

Annie held out her arms to him, resting her hands on his shoulders. He told her when to jump, and she felt the working of the muscle under his shirt as he lifted her over to shore. Then he splashed out after her.

Ellie was sitting on a fallen log, peeling back her socks to look at her ankles.

"What are you looking for?" Annie asked.

"Leeches," Ellie said. "The water up this inlet is a mixture of salt and fresh from a spring on the island that runs into the sea here. It's fresh enough for some seriously nasty leeches."

"Great," Ian said. He shone his own light on the bottoms of his pant legs, poking at his socks. Thankfully he wasn't carrying any blood-sucking passengers. "So—do we wait here for morning?"

Ellie nodded. "Yeah. The island isn't really safe in the dark."

"Not safe how?" Annie asked.

"You could walk into a tree," Ellie said with a shrug. "Or get bit by a snake. Or fall in a hole. Some of the buildings are down to foundations."

Annie peered out into the darkness pressing around them. She heard a rustle of bushes and stepped closer to Ian. He put a warm arm around her. "Probably just a possum," he said quietly. "Or a raccoon."

Or deadly poisonous snake, Annie thought with a shiver, and she hoped that dawn came early—really early.

$$\sim 13 \sim$$

I told no one about the old woman, not even my mother—
though she suspected something horrible had happened on the
street as I was not in the habit of soiling myself, turning pale
with fear and shaking like a wet dog. She refused to take me
back to the island that night and rented a room in the village.
She sent word to my father that she was overwrought from
the horrible circumstances surrounding my great-grandfather's
death. She told him she would not set foot on the island again.
She was wrong.

—Steven Fuller, 1925

Annie jumped again at a rustle behind her. She turned and saw Ellie hauling a small rucksack into her lap. The girl pulled out bottles of water and granola bars. "You guys want some? I brought enough for all of us."

"Thanks," Annie said, taking a bottle of water. "That was very thoughtful."

Ellie shrugged. "I come out here a lot. It's a good place to think, but you gotta bring your own snacks."

"If you come out here a lot," Annie asked. "do you know of anything on this island that folks would want to keep secret?"

Ellie shook her head. "No. It's just old buildings. I mean, some of them are kinda cool and spooky, but there's nothing valuable in them. I don't really wander around the island much. Mostly I stay near here. It's quiet, and like I said, it's a good place to think."

"Could someone be using the island for some kind of secret activity?" Ian asked. "Maybe something illegal?"

"I don't know what it could be," Ellie said. "Especially to get Uncle Bob involved. My uncle is *not* a criminal."

"Well, whatever might be hidden on the island," Ian said, "we can't start looking until daylight. We might as well be comfortable while we wait." He looked around a moment before walking over to a large rock, half-covered in brambles. He took his jacket off and wrapped it around his forearm so he could clear the thorny vines. Then he spread the jacket on the top of the rock. "Care to join me, Annie?"

"After all that work, how could I say no?" Annie walked over and sat as far to one side of the jacket as possible to make room for Ian. Still, when he sat, his leg pressed close to hers and his broad shoulders seemed unusually wide.

Ian unscrewed the top of his water bottle and took a long drink. They sat quietly, listening to the sound of insects and frogs in the night. Now and then something would rustle in the bushes, but there were no howls, barks, or other sounds to suggest there could be dogs on the island.

"You said you come out here often," Annie said, turning to Ellie. "I watched a video of two people who were on the island at night. They ran away when they heard dogs. It's clear on the video."

Ellie shrugged. "I've never heard dogs here."

"So there couldn't be wild dogs?" Ian asked.

"We have trouble sometimes with feral dogs on the mainland," Ellie said. "Idiot tourists dump dogs and cats at the end of summer. And a lot of guys around here aren't big on the whole 'spay and neuter' thing. Still, to get to the island, they'd have to swim over from the mainland, and I don't know what would draw them."

"It sounds like there are animals on the island," Annie said.

"Sure, raccoons and opossums," Ellie answered. "Maybe some pigs, even though I've never seen any. But we have those in the woods around Preacher's Reach. Why come out here to find something that's more plentiful where you are?"

"No one ever brings dogs over to hunt?" Ian asked.

"Again, easier hunting on the mainland," Ellie said.

"What if they hunt out of season?" Ian asked. "You could do it easier over here."

"It's not that hard anywhere," Ellie said. "With money being what it is ... well, you've seen the town. Some folks hunt and fish just to keep meat on the table. No one has the heart to police it really hard right now."

Dawn came slowly, unnoticed until Annie suddenly realized she could see colors again—the faded blue of Ellie's jeans and the green of the surrounding foliage. It was morning and time for them to hunt for clues.

Ellie led them through the woods, and Annie immediately recognized it as a daylight version of the Internet video with thick undergrowth. The island had trails, but they were badly overgrown, and Ellie seemed to find them by instinct as much as anything else. Annie watched her feet closely, watching for the snakes Ellie had mentioned.

"The first buildings are just up ahead," Ellie said after they'd been walking for a while.

Annie saw that they'd come at the buildings from a different angle than the one on the video. The building they faced wasn't made of cinder blocks; it was brick, now crumbling. They walked straight at the long, low brick building. Vines covered the building so thickly that the door opening looked like a cave with the corners rounded by the tangle of growth clinging to the bricks around the frame. Here and there, portions of windows—most with cracked or missing glass—peeked out from behind vine shutters. They walked to the doorway and looked in.

This was one of the buildings with little or no roof left. Inside, the broken roof had let in seeds and sun, making the undergrowth inside the building nearly as thick as that on the outside. Support columns held up nothing but sky and cracked crossbeams.

Bare spots on the floor showed half-rotted boards. "It's beautiful and horrible at the same time," Annie said quietly.

"It also looks deadly," Ian added. He turned to Ellie. "Have you been in there?"

She shrugged. "Once, with some friends. The floor-board fell through over there." She pointed to a spot where the undergrowth looked a bit less thick. "One of the guys fell through and broke his leg. We had to get rope and pull him out. We got in so much trouble for that."

"Do you think Jim and Alice could be in there?" Annie asked, taking a step into the building. "Down in that hole?"

Ian quickly reached out and caught Annie's arm. "I think I don't want you to end up down there."

"What are we doing here if we're not going to look?" Annie asked.

"I have an idea," Ellie said. "If you want ... ."

"What?" Ian said, his tone reluctant.

"I brought rope," Ellie said. "We could rope together and one of us could walk that way. Close enough to look, anyway. If there are people down there, you'd see."

"OK," Ian said. "I'll go."

Ellie shook her head. "Not a good idea. You weigh the most. You're gonna go through the floor easier and be way harder for us to hold onto. It needs to be someone light. I reckon I'm the lightest, and I've been in there before."

"I don't like you taking that kind of risk," Ian said.

Ellie shrugged. "It's the best idea, but you'll need to walk in partway," she said to Annie. "We need to rope together in short lengths so that we have the leverage to keep us out of the basement if the floor breaks."

Ian was shaking his head as Annie said, "Fine. I can do that."

"No," Ian told her.

"I'll be following Ellie," Annie said. "So I'll be walking on boards that already held her. I don't weigh that much more than she does. I'll be fine."

Ian made a frustrated sound that reminded Annie a bit of a growl, but he helped them rope together, checking the knots carefully. "You've had some practice with this," he told Ellie.

"I do a little rock climbing," she said.

Annie smiled. "You like adventure."

Ellie nodded, smiling a little herself. "Yeah."

"You remind me of Alice," Annie said. "She was always coming up with ideas to get us half-killed when we were young."

Ellie laughed. "Billy says that about me sometimes."

Finally the ropes were secure, and Ellie began her careful walk into the room. Annie's job was to keep the rope between them taunt while still letting the girl move. She also watched where Ellie put her feet, knowing she'd have to walk in those footsteps as soon as the rope ran out.

When it did, Ellie looked over her shoulder and called out. "The floor is pretty good at first, but it gets kinda spongy after about ten feet. Be sure to keep taunt then."

Annie nodded, too nervous to speak. She stepped out into the room. As Ellie said, the floor felt firm under the rope of vines. She still moved slowly and carefully. With each step Annie took, Ellie took one forward toward the open spot in the floor.

The passage across the room went painfully slow, and Annie could feel the pounding of her heart. "OK," Ellie finally called. "I can see the hole, but the floor is bad here. I can't go much closer. Hold tight, Mrs. Dawson!"

They moved in inches then, and Annie could see Ellie leaning forward, searching into the darkness. "I'm going to have to use my flashlight," the girl said. She fished in her shirt pocket for the small LED flashlight. "I don't see anyone."

"Come on back," Ian urged.

"I think I can move a little closer," Ellie said.

"Just come on back!"

Annie felt the pull of the rope as Ellie crept closer by inches again. Suddenly the rope jerked hard forward in her hands at the same time that Ellie shrieked. Annie held on tight and threw herself backwards. She felt the answering jerk of the rope around her as Ian hauled her backwards hard. That's going to leave a mark, Annie thought as the rope tightened painfully around her ribs.

Annie was almost sitting, scooting backwards slowly as Ian continued to pull.

"I'm OK," Ellie called. "The floor gave but y'all caught me. I'm not hurt."

"Time for everyone to get out of there," Ian said.

"Coming," Ellie said. "You can stop pulling so hard. I need to breathe."

Annie stood again, letting the rope slack slightly in her hands, the rope around her middle still felt uncomfortably firm, but she wasn't being dragged toward the door anymore.

As Ellie moved back toward Annie, Annie backed toward the door to keep the rope fairly taunt. Finally they were all outside the building again. That's when Annie noticed Ellie held something in her hand. "What's that?" Annie said.

"It's what I was going after when the floor crumbled away under me," Ellie said, handing a bit of soft fabric to Annie. "It was caught up in some of the vines."

Annie held the light scarf in trembling hands. She recognized it. It was one of the ones Alice often wore to keep her hair from flying around too much when she was driving her convertible. She looked up at Ian. "It's Alice's," she said. "She could be in that hole."

"I don't think so," Ellie said. "I got a pretty clear view of the hole when I was about to fall into it. There's some kind of cinder-block room down there, but it's not all that big. I would have noticed a person in it."

Annie sighed in relief. "Still, Alice was in here. This is

definitely her scarf. Someone should come back with the equipment to really look down there."

"We'll show it to Chief Harper," Ian said.

"Just keep my name out of it," Ellie said. "I do not want any trouble from this."

"We promise," Annie said. "But I'm not done looking. We found one clue. There could be others."

They waded through the brush to circle the brick building. On the other side, they found a narrow paved road leading away from the building. The pavement was covered with sticks and rotting leaves, but still offered the best walking they'd had since stepping onto the island.

Ahead, they saw more brick buildings. One had a row of small windows and a tall chimney. The other was two stories with tall arched windows on the lower floor and smaller ones on the upper. Ellie led the way toward the buildings. "I've been in both of these," she said. "They're in better shape, though the stairs are horrible in that one. The third big building—the main house—is further down the road."

"Do you know what the buildings were used for?" Annie asked.

Ellie shrugged. "There's not much left in them, but there are some old metal beds in that one." She pointed to the two-story building. "So I guess people slept there."

They walked to the doorway of the long one-story building and looked inside. "I think this might have been a carriage house originally," Ian said. "Or a stable, but clearly it's been used for something else later." A long metal table in one part of the room seemed held together by rust and spiderwebs. Other rusted heaps of metal hid their original uses in their decay.

They backed out of the doorway and walked to the two-story building. The structure was in terrible shape with the ground around it littered with bricks that had fallen out, leaving dark gaps in the walls. In places, the wooden window frames had twisted, pulling away from the wall and hanging loose. If there was an unbroken pane of glass, Annie couldn't see it.

They stepped carefully over the brick and entered the covered passage that led to the door. Ian looked warily at the roof over their head, as if expecting it to fall on them at any second. Surprisingly, the building still had an intact door, though it had warped into the frame. Ian had to put his shoulder to it, pushing hard to scoot it open enough for them to slip in. "Be careful of the floor," he warned.

The floors were filthy and littered with plaster that had fallen from the walls, but they felt solid. The place was a maze of small rooms with narrow beds. Each room had a metal washstand with metal shelves mounted on the wall over it.

"Patient rooms?" Annie suggested.

"Maybe," Ian agreed.

They walked down a hall that opened into a more spacious foyer, though the walls were just as broken, showing lathe strips everywhere. A wrought-iron spiral staircase offered access to the upstairs. The stairs and railing were uniformly covered in flaking rust, but under the rust, the beauty of the hand-forged metal was still visible.

"Is it safe to climb?" Annie asked.

"I don't know," Ellie said. "After seeing someone fall through a floor, I never went up any of the stairs anywhere."

Annie walked close and peered up. Ian shook the railing, but it didn't move. He stomped the bottom step, but it held under his feet. "I'll go take a look."

"I'll come with you," Annie said.

Ian turned to give her a look, but Annie merely smiled at him. Finally he sighed and started up the stairs. "I'll just stay here," Ellie said.

The upstairs offered more rooms but no more signs of Jim and Alice. They walked back down carefully. "So now there's just the main house?" Ian asked.

"I think so," Ellie said. "These are all the buildings I've ever seen."

"Then we better head for there next."

They walked down the littered road. Once they broke free of the thickest overgrowth, they spotted the house. It must have been lovely at one time. It was red brick like the outbuildings, but the entrance was a lovely arched brick with what must have been white trim. More arches marked a narrow veranda on one side with tall windows behind it. On the other side of the entrance, a bay window jutted out toward them with more of the tall windows. Both the veranda and the bay window had narrow railings above them, as if to allow access from the second floor onto their roofs.

"This looks like it's in much better shape," Annie said.

"Before I was born, people say there was talk of restoring it or something," Ellie said. "I think some folks still come out and hack at the kudzu once in a while. Least it looks like it. I've never seen anyone out here."

That alone made it mysterious enough to give Annie hope. They walked to the entrance door. Two screen doors, their paint chipped and frames slightly bent, helped protect the nicer wooden doors beyond. Tall windows on either side of the doors held completely intact glass. "That's almost spooky," Annie said, pointing at the glass.

Ian opened one of the screen doors and tried the door beyond. It was locked, not just stuck. The other door was equally unresponsive. "We'll have to find another way in," he said.

They circled the house where a white-painted side porch jutted well away from the tall windows of the rooms beyond. Annie walked to one window and peered in. The room looked empty and far less strewn with rubble than the other buildings.

At the back of the house, they found another door. This one opened with some brute force from Ian. They stepped into the old kitchen. The many windows brought light into the room, making it almost cheery despite the rust and decay. They walked through the rooms of the house quietly. Though all showed signs of neglect in chipping paint and plaster, they also hinted at the original beauty of the house with its carved fireplace mantels and beautiful dark wooden trim.

Though beautiful, the house was also clearly empty. Finally they trooped back down to the kitchen. As they walked toward the door, Annie stopped. Something near the old cast-iron stove had caught her eye. Whatever it was shone a bit in the light, and the black paint on the stove itself was far too old to shine.

"What are you looking at?" Ian asked as Annie walked toward the stove and bent down.

"I'm not sure," Annie slipped her hand under the ornate edge of the stove, shuddering at the soft brush of cobwebs. Her hand touched something smooth, and she pulled it out. It was a cane. She held it up. "This is Jim's cane. I recognize it."

Ian reached out and touched the head of the cane. "There's something on it. Something dark red and crusty."

"Eww!" Ellie exclaimed as she leaned in between them to peer at it. "Do you think that's blood?"

"I think it might be," Ian said. "And I think Chief Harper might need to take a much closer look at this island."

Annie looked in horror at the head of the cane. "Blood?" she whispered.

"Don't panic," Ian told her. "If that's what it is, there isn't much of it. It mostly tells us Jim was here."

"He doesn't exactly get around well without his cane," Annie said. "Leaving it behind is bad. You know it is."

"It's not good," Ian agreed. "But let's take this one step at a time. It's time to go to the police." He turned to Ellie. "I know you don't want your boat seen, but we need to go back to the mainland *now*."

Ellie looked at the cane, then nodded grimly. "What are a few years of being grounded?"

~ 14 ~

My father was afraid. I knew that from listening behind the sofa. Still, he was not a man who admitted fear easily. The Fullers were soldiers, leaders, men of action and valor. Father would not see himself differently, even when the thought of a curse haunted his own dreams as much as it did mine. He came to the mainland the next day and insisted Mother and I return to the island. He wasn't fooled by Mother's insistence that it was her fears that kept us away. One look at me told the truth. I was terrified!

—Steven Fuller, 1925

The ride back to the mainland was made mostly in silence. For one thing, seeing Ellie's boat in the clear light of daylight left Ian speechless. Annie doubted Ian would let either of them get in that particular boat again. On top of that, the blood on Jim's cane brought fresh worry about him and Alice. And Annie suspected Ellie had worries of her own. The teenager watched the shoreline sharply as they crossed back.

Once they landed, Annie thanked Ellie and promised not to mention her name when they spoke with the police. Then she and Ian left for the police department. They found Doris looking as thrilled to see them as she had on their previous visit.

"We would like to speak with Chief Harper," Ian said. "We have some things he needs to see."

She looked at them silently for a moment, and Annie could almost hear her preparing to refuse, but finally she slipped off her stool. "I'll see if he's available," she said over her shoulder as she disappeared.

Just as Annie was beginning to wonder if Doris had simply slipped out a back door to leave them standing in the lobby forever, the heavy-set woman huffed back to her stool, and one of the doors opened to reveal Chief Harper. If anything, the older man looked thinner and more tired than when they'd spoken to him before.

"So, still in our fair town?" he asked pleasantly.

"We've been out to Fuller's Island," Ian said. "And we found a scarf belonging to Alice MacFarlane. We also found Jim Parker's cane. There's something on this cane, and we're thinking it might be blood."

Chief Harper raised an eyebrow and took the cane from Ian. He looked it over closely, sniffing the dried splotches. "Could be," he said. "Maybe someone used it to drive one of the local possums out of their pantry. They're nearly as bad as raccoons, just not as smart."

"Maybe you could have your lab test it?" Annie asked. "To see if it's human."

The chief laughed. "This isn't an episode of *CSI*, lady. We don't have a lab, unless you count our local pharmacy. Heck, the closest thing we have to a coroner is the vet. How do you know this is Jim Parker's cane?"

"I've seen him with it," Annie said.

The chief looked over the cane. "It's not especially fancy. I imagine lots of folks have this cane."

"Surely you're not going to ignore evidence," Annie said.

"Evidence of what?" the chief asked. "That they were on the island? We know they were on the island. Bob Maynard rented them a boat for the day, and they brought it back. If your friend lost her scarf or your other friend beat a snake to death with his cane, that's not evidence of anything we didn't already know—they were on the island. But my man searched, and they're not on the island any more."

"You won't even go back out there?" Ian asked.

"I'll send someone back out to look again," the chief said. "As soon as I can spare a man to beat bushes on an empty island, looking for adult tourists who didn't know they were supposed to check in with *dad*. And I'll get back to you if you're still in town."

"Thanks so much," Ian said, his voice nearly dripping with sarcasm.

"You're welcome," the chief said. "And as long as we're exchanging thanks—thanks for getting Nora Harlow all het up. That woman can wear out a rock when she thinks she's chasing a story for that newspaper of hers."

"Good for Nora," Annie said. "I'll have to thank her."

"Well, why don't you rush along and do that," the chief said, handing Ian back the battered cane. "And I'll let you know when we search the island again."

Ian was shaking his head in amazement as they left. "I can't believe the chief cares so little about the disappearance of two people."

"Two *tourists*," Annie said. "Do you think he's in on covering this up?"

"I don't know," Ian said. "He may truly just not care."

"Well, I'm glad to know that Nora apparently does," Annie said. "Maybe we could go see her after we change. I smell like a swamp."

Ian leaned close and sniffed Annie's hair. "Still smells like sunshine and peaches to me."

Annie looked at him in surprise. "I don't use peach shampoo."

"Must just be you then," he said.

She shook her head. "I never know when you're being charming or just teasing me."

Ian took Annie's hand and tucked it into the crook of his arm as he walked. "Whichever one you like better, that's the one I was going for," he said.

When they reached the inn, they found Mary Beth sitting on the porch. She hopped up as soon as the SUV turned into the drive, hurrying out to the car. "I'm so glad to see you both," she said. "But I didn't expect you back until dark."

"We found some things," Annie said. "And we came back early thinking we could get the police to do a more serious search."

"You've been to the police again?" Mary Beth said.

"For as much good as it did us," Annie answered, her voice angry.

"The chief isn't taking this seriously," Ian added as he walked around the car to join them. "Or else he's hiding things."

"So what did you find?" Mary Beth said.

"Alice's scarf and Jim's cane," Annie answered. Then she took a deep breath. "We think there is blood on the cane."

Mary Beth gasped. "Blood. And the police don't care?"

"We don't know whose blood it is," Ian answered, "or even what kind of blood it is. We need more allies around here. Ellie helped, but she's barely more than a child."

"But from something Chief Harper said, we think Nora Harlow might help," Annie said.

Mary Beth nodded, still looking a little stunned. Together they began to walk toward the inn, so Mary Beth dropped her voice. "That's a lot to take in. I've been poking around here, looking for Alice and Jim's luggage, but nothing so far. And Stella has been a little busy."

"Busy?" Annie said.

"Apparently Mrs. Ayers has a big brother," Mary Beth said, a smile creeping over her face. "He showed up at breakfast, and he's quite taken with Stella."

"Our Stella?" Annie repeated. "How's she handling it."

"At first, she was appalled," Mary Beth said. "But when he offered to take her on the tour of the inn and grounds—well, it sounded like the perfect chance to hunt for luggage."

"How did that go?" Annie asked.

"It's still going." Mary Beth nodded pointedly toward the back grounds of the inn. Annie looked in the direction she indicated and spotted Stella walking at the side of a tall white-haired man who had Stella's hand tucked in the crook of his arm, much like Annie had walked with Ian in the police parking lot.

"He's handsome," Annie said with a grin.

"And charming," Mary Beth added.

Just then Stella must have caught sight of them standing together in the parking lot. She waved, and then gestured for them to come join her. Annie leaned close to Mary Beth as they walked. "Do I smell like a swamp?" she asked. "I keep smelling it."

Mary Beth took a quick sniff and shook her head. "No, you're fine," she looked over at Ian. "Maybe it's Ian. His pant legs look a little suspicious."

Annie glanced down at Ian's lower pant leg, remembering the sound of him splashing into the swampy water. The denim was definitely darker from just above his knees to his feet. And his shoes were disgusting. Annie realized *that's* where the smell was coming from.

They reached Stella just as their friend gently slipped her hand free of Mrs. Ayer's brother. "Charles, I'd like you to meet my friends Annie Dawson and Ian Butler," Stella said. "Ian is the mayor of Stony Point." Ian nodded at the older man, and Annie could see they were nearly eye to eye. "Annie, Ian, I'd like you to meet Charles Bonneau. He's Mrs. Ayers's brother."

"Pleased to meet you," Charles Bonneau said, bowing slightly. "I've always thought the South had the most lovely ladies in the world, but Stella has proved my theory incorrect. And now I see still more evidence with you, Mrs. Dawson."

"Well, technically, I spent more years living in Texas than Maine," Annie said, raising an eyebrow at the older man's shameless flattery.

"Charles and I found the oddest thing in the back outbuilding," Stella said. "Several pieces of luggage. They were tucked behind some old boards. We're on the way to ask his sister about it."

"It does seem an odd place to store unclaimed luggage," Charles said. "We need to move it inside before the weather destroys it."

"That is odd," Annie said. "Maybe we could all hear what Mrs. Ayers says?"

"Why on earth would you be interested in unclaimed luggage?" Charles asked. "I'm certain we're not having an auction."

"We have two friends who have gone missing," Ian said. "We know they stayed here. If the pieces you saw belong to them, we're very interested."

"My friend had lovely luggage," Annie said. "A matched set. I saw it several times. The suitcases had a floral brocade pattern."

"Then it sounds like we may indeed have found your friend's luggage," Charles said. "Let us go and see if Suzanne can enlighten us about this."

The tall man's straight posture and long-limbed stride made him seem much younger than his lined face implied. He led them through a back door of the inn that opened into a small mudroom. He kept walking, and they entered a large kitchen. He called, "Suzanne! Are you back here?"

Mrs. Ayers raised up from where she had been pulling pans out of a cupboard. "I'm right here, Charles. You don't need to bellow." When she caught sight of Annie and the rest, she froze. "Charles, do you have to drag guests through the private parts of the house?"

"I was giving the lovely Mrs. Brickson a tour," Charles said. "And we found some luggage in the back outbuilding. Apparently it belongs to friends of these people."

Mrs. Ayers looked alarmed but recovered quickly. "The luggage belonged to a couple who left suddenly without checking out. I was hoping they would return to claim the luggage and help settle on exactly how much they owe. I'm not really a storage company."

"So Alice MacFarlane and Jim Parker did stay here," Annie said.

"Yes," Mrs. Ayers answered. "They checked in, spent the night in the two downstairs rooms, went on some sort of excursion the next morning, and didn't return. I left their rooms open for a couple days and called the lady's cellphone number, but it rolled to voice mail. Then I opened the rooms to rent again."

"So you say they only stayed one night," Annie said.

"I say it because it's true," Mrs. Ayers answered.

"Why didn't you say this before we found the luggage?" Mary Beth asked.

Mrs. Ayers put her hands on her hips, her voice firm. "You didn't ask about your friends until just now."

"But you didn't tell Chief Edwards when he called from Stony Point either," Ian said. "He called all of the inns in and around Preacher's Reach and reported that every single one said Jim and Alice had not stayed with them.

"I do not know what you're talking about," Mrs. Ayers

snapped. "No one called. No one asked. And I don't like your tone."

Charles raised his hands and spoke to his sister in consoling tones. "We all need to calm down a bit," he said. "We should bring the luggage into the inn—storing it in the outbuilding is a dreadful idea anyway. Between the weather and the vermin, the luggage would be covered in mold and tattered in a week. We'll bring it in and open it up."

"We certainly will not," Mrs. Ayers said. "We have no proof these people are friends of those others. I will not be sued by someone for poking around in their luggage."

"Didn't you have to pack the bags when you took them from the room?" asked Annie.

"No," she said. "They were completely packed. I just moved them."

"Clearly we have a mystery here," Charles said, rubbing his hands together eagerly. "And since I own this inn just slightly more than you do, dear sister. I'm going to overrule you. We'll bring in the luggage and check it out!"

"Charles!" Mrs. Ayers nearly shouted. "We will not."

"She was always bossy," he said to Stella. "Come on, let's go and get the bags."

He spun and marched back out the back door and across the back lawn. His sister followed close behind him, shouting at him the whole way, but he paid her no more attention than he would give a buzzing insect. Annie and the others followed the brother and sister to the outbuilding.

Ian stepped forward to help Charles lift the bags from behind the stacked boards. Annie could clearly see the boards had been arranged to help conceal the luggage.

When she saw the floral pattern on two of the bags, she said, "Those are definitely Alice's."

By this point, Mrs. Ayers had resorted to swatting her brother on the arm, but he still ignored her. His face was alight with the excitement of solving the mystery. He handed two of the bags to Ian and carried the other two himself. "Let's take these inside and see what secrets they have."

The men carried the bags indoors, and Stella offered her room as a quiet place to search the bags. Charles gave her a rakish grin. "I was hoping to see your room, dear lady," he said. "This isn't quite the way I had hoped to see it, but it's very exciting just the same."

Stella seemed speechless at this bit of flirting and just led them to the room silently, her cheeks unusually pink. The men set the bags on the floor, and Charles fetched towels from the bathroom to spread out on the bed quilt to place the bags on. The outside of the luggage was soiled and cobwebby from their days in the shed.

When Ian unzipped Alice's large bag, Annie gasped. She knew her friend was a neat and organized packer. It's one of the things Alice was especially proud of. But the contents of the bag were crammed. Alice's blouses were wrinkled, and someone had put a dirty pair of shoes on top of the clean clothes. The whole bag stunk of the same smell Ian had carried back from Fuller's Island.

"Whew," Mary Beth said. "They stink like swamp."

"Which means they came back from the island," Annie said, turning to look at Mrs. Ayers. "They came back with dirty swamp-stained clothes. And Alice didn't pack this bag.

She wouldn't treat her things this way."

"Suzanne," Charles said, his face puzzled, "what is going on here? Did you pack this bag? Are there things you need to tell us?"

"I told you all I know about the bags," Mrs. Ayers said, backing away from the group. "And if those people create any trouble, it's on your head, Charles. I tried." She spun and stalked out of the room.

"We should go after her," Mary Beth said, "and shake the truth out of her."

"I wouldn't normally be in favor of acting like ruffians," Stella said, "but I would make an exception in this case."

"I would shake her for you," Charles said, "if it would do any good at all. Suzanne has been stubborn since she was a child. I once saw her hold her breath until she passed out." He shook his head. "I don't think you'll get any answers from her. But I don't know what's going on. Suzanne is stubborn, but she's not a dishonest person."

"Someone is scaring people out of talking to us," Annie said, "and out of helping us. Your sister isn't the only one lying in Preacher's Reach. What do you know about Fuller's Island?"

"Fuller's Island?" Charles looked surprised. "It's deserted. There are all sorts of silly ghost stories attached to it. It was *the* place for teenaged boys to prove their courage to shrieking girlfriends at one time. But mostly it's not really very interesting, unless you like watching bricks fall out of walls."

"You've been there?" Stella asked.

"My dear, at one time or another, nearly everyone at

Preacher's Reach has been there," he grinned. "As I said, it was the place for young men to take their young ladies. You'd be amazed how pleasant it is to have some trembling girl fling herself on you when you're a young man."

"It's also the place where our friends went," Annie said. "And the last place we know of them being."

"They disappeared on the island?" Charles asked.

"We believe so," Ian said. "We know they were there several times over the course of a few days. We don't know much else."

"Have you spoken with Chief Harper?" Charles asked.

"He wasn't a lot of help," Ian said dryly.

Charles sighed. "He can be a bit lazy. He likes it best when no one rocks the boat too much."

"So far, you're almost the only one who's been help-ful," Annie said. "You and Nora Harlow." She didn't mention Ellie, since the girl had been so worried about being found helping them.

"Nora? Beatrice's daughter?" Charles said. "I hear she's grown up to be a fine girl."

"We're hoping she can help us get back out to the island," Ian said.

"Back?" Charles echoed.

"We were out there this morning," Ian said. "But we're *not* traveling the same way again."

"Well, if it's a boat you're needing," Charles said, "maybe I can help. I could call around and see what I can find. Though I don't know how much help I'll be in storm-ing the island and rescuing your friends. I'm a little old for heroics."

"If you can help us get a boat, you'll be hero enough for me," Annie said.

"Thank you, dear," Charles said. He turned to smile mischievously at Stella. "But will I be hero enough for you?"

"I'll let you know," Stella said.

Charles's smile grew. "Then just let me make some calls."

~ 15 ~

Mother was not a malleable woman. She lacked the soft weakness that a woman of her station was expected to have. I believe Father admired that in her. But even so, she was ultimately subject to my father's wishes, and he wished her to return to the island. He wished me to face my fears. I believe he meant it for my good. I believe it was also to be his redemption. His own fears shamed him. If we stood together against the stories, against the curse, then he would feel like a Fuller again—and feel as if he had done right by me as well.

—Steven Fuller, 1925

While Charles settled down in Stella's room to make some calls under Stella and Mary Beth's watchful eyes, Annie and Ian headed upstairs to shower and change. Annie wanted to track down Nora Harlow as soon as they were free of the swamp stink. She had the feeling they needed all the allies they could get.

They finally headed out to the newspaper office where they found Nora scribbling notes on paper and eating a sandwich. "Hey," she said, her face lighting up when she saw them. "I think I found us a boat!"

"Great," Annie said. "We've found a few things too."

"Oh?" Nora's glance sharpened, and she scooted a fresh piece of paper out of the pile. With pen poised over paper, she looked at Annie expectantly. "Shoot!"

"We went out to the island," Annie said.

Nora's eyebrows went up in surprise, but she didn't ask any questions and just waited for Annie to continue.

"We found one of Alice's scarves and a cane that I know belongs to Jim," Annie said. "The cane has blood on it, or something that looks a lot like blood."

"That sounds bad," Nora said. "Have you told Chief Harper?"

"He was less than alarmed," Ian said. "He promised to send someone out to check the island again, when he got around to it."

Nora shook her head. "He's been stonewalling me too. People are acting weird. People I wouldn't expect it of."

"We found something else too," Annie said. "Alice and Jim's luggage. It was stashed in a shed on the Preacher's Rest property. Mrs. Ayers said they just left it behind, all packed up—but we looked in the suitcases. Alice wouldn't have just thrown her things into a bag the way they were. And there was swamp mud on one of her pairs of shoes."

"Curiouser and curiouser," Nora said. "We need to get back out to the island. My friend can let me use his boat tomorrow, but then he has to have it back. He heads down to the Florida Keys for the winter, and it's time for him to go. I got him to postpone a day, but that's all we get."

"We'll be ready," Ian said.

"For now, I'm heading over to Bob Maynard's boat rentals," Nora said. "I've known him all my life. If he's going to lie to me, he needs to do it to my face."

"Can we come?" Annie asked.

"You'd be welcome," Nora said.

On the ride out to the boat rental, Nora asked more questions about Jim and Alice, taking notes as Annie spoke. Ian threw in a remark now and then, but mostly he concentrated on driving.

Nora laughed out loud when Annie told her what had started Jim's interest in the island. "*The Fuller Family History*?" she asked. "I read that years ago. My mom has a copy in her collection. That guy was a piece of work. The whole family sounded a little whacko in the book."

"He certainly seemed to take the curse very seriously," Annie said.

"Of course," Nora added generously, "He was just a little kid when all that curse garbage started."

"So you don't think the family was cursed?" Ian asked.

"Even my mom doesn't totally buy the curse," Nora said. "And she thinks Preacher's Reach is visited by aliens regularly. Now, I believe some of the old local families were into some strange stuff. There's a belief in witchy stuff that goes way back in a lot of Southern bloodlines. Folks brought all that stuff from Europe; they mixed it in with different mystical beliefs that run all through this area. Basically, the South loves ghost stories."

"But you're less open-minded?" Ian asked.

"I tend to believe in what I can see," Nora said. "But I like to listen. And I love a good story. At any rate, whatever is keeping your friends from getting back to you, I don't think it's ghosts or devil dogs."

"I don't think it is either," Ian said.

"Do you still have that cane?" Nora asked.

"Yes, the chief was less than interested in examining it," Ian said.

"I know someone who could run some tests on the blood," Nora said. "I think she could tell us for sure if it was blood and maybe if it was human blood. She's a biology teacher at the high school, but she was a researcher before that."

"A researcher turned high school teacher?" Ian asked.

Nora shrugged. "She got homesick and said she was tired of the politics of research. Of course, now she has to deal with the politics of teaching."

"We have the cane in the back of the car," Annie said. "Maybe we can take it to your friend after we talk to Bob Maynard."

"Excellent idea," Nora said.

As they pulled into the parking lot at the boat rental, Bob Maynard walked out on the narrow porch of the building to scowl at them. As soon as Ian stepped out of the vehicle, Bob called, "I told you, I don't have any boats to rent!"

"We're actually here for something else," Ian said.

Annie and Nora walked around from the passenger side of the vehicle. Bob Maynard tensed at the sight of them. "Nora," he said with a nod.

"Bob Maynard," she said. "You want to tell me why you're lying to folks? Including me?"

The man's face darkened in anger. "I don't like being called a liar."

"Then don't tell lies," Nora said as she marched up on the porch and stared up into his face. "Why did you tell these folks that you only rented the boat to their friends one day when it was several? And why did you tell them their friends dropped the boat off at night when you had to go over to the island to retrieve it?"

"What makes you think all that?" he growled back at her.

"I don't think it," she said. "I know it."

"Nora," Bob said, his voice dropping a bit. "You don't know what kinda hornet's nest you're kicking."

"Well, I figure if I keep kicking it hard enough, something will come buzzing out," she said. "Then I'll know."

"Fat lot of good knowing will do you," Bob said.

"I've never known you to be a coward before," Nora said.

He snorted. "I've certainly known you to be a pain in the ... ."

She held up a hand. "We're wandering off topic. What's making you tell lies, Bob? What are you scared of?"

"I'm not scared of anything ... for me," he said. "I have more to worry about than my own hide, Nora. You know I got my little sister's kid to think about."

"Yes, I do," Nora said, looking around. "Where is little Ellie? I haven't seen her in a while. I should say hi."

"She's not here right now," Bob said. "She's gone to visit with her daddy's people down Florida way."

"Really?" Annie said, shocked. "When did she leave?"

"Not that it's any of your nosy business, but just an hour or so ago," Bob said. "She's been missing them real bad lately."

Annie glanced at Ian. It seemed unlikely that Ellie would suddenly decide to pay a visit to her relatives exactly when they got back from the island. She must have been caught helping them. She just hoped the teenager really was safe and sound with family.

"Look, Bob," Nora said. "I'm going to find out what's going on with or without your help. I just thought we'd been friends long enough to make it *with*."

He shook his head. "I can't help you, Nora, except to give you some advice. You need to decide what's more important to you—family or some crazy tourists. Because you got more to lose than just you."

Nora's eyes widened, and she launched herself at Bob. "How dare you threaten my mother!"

Bob caught her by both arms. "I'm not threatening anyone, Nora. Not me." He shook her slightly, but then let go of her as Ian closed the distance between them. Bob took his hands off Nora gently. "Not me."

Annie tugged at Nora's arm. "I don't think we're going to get anywhere here, Nora. We should go do our next errand."

Nora reluctantly tore her stare away from Bob and let Annie lead her to the car.

Bob shook his head as Annie and Nora climbed in the car. He looked at Ian, and for a moment, his gaze was stricken. "Look after her."

"I'll do what I can," Ian said. "You're not helping much."

"It would help her the most if you could get her to stop," Bob said. "If you could get both of them to stop."

"They'll stop when we get our friends back," Ian said. Then he lowered his voice. "Is your niece all right? Is she really with family?"

"She's not your concern," Bob said, his voice

turning cold again, and then he turned and walked into the building.

With no way to pry more information from the man, Ian sighed and headed for the vehicle. Nora fumed for a while as they drove out of the dense swampy forest, but eventually calmed enough to give them directions to the school.

Annie glanced at her watch. "School's been over for a while hasn't it?"

"Yeah," Nora said. "But Jen handles after-school detention most of the time, so she'll still be there."

The school was a single-story building that looked a bit like a spider with long-legged hallways heading off the main building in all directions. Nora bypassed the main entrance and walked along the sidewalk to the end of one of the wings. They found the door propped open with a rock. "The kids do that," Nora said. "It lets them sneak out and smoke if Jen takes a bathroom break during detention."

"Does that happen often?" Annie asked.

"Not since Jen figured out what was going on," Nora said. "But teenaged hope springs eternal."

As they walked down the hall, a sudden rush of teenagers poured out of a room and practically ran them over. "Detention must be over," Ian said as he pulled Annie safely to one side. As soon as the stampede passed, they walked into the large classroom. A round-faced young woman with olive skin and long straight black hair looked toward them, blinking brown eyes behind over-large glasses.

"Jen," Nora said, "I have some people I want you to meet." She quickly introduced Ian and Annie. Then added, "I have a huge favor to ask."

"Sure," Jen said, squinting slightly at her friend. "What can I do for you?"

"First," Nora said, "what's with the owl imitation? You look about half-blind."

Jen sighed. "My contacts were bothering my eyes, and I left my glasses at Andrew's place. So I had to wear these and they're old—really old—so not exactly the right prescription any more."

"Well, don't forget to collect your glasses before he leaves for the Keys. And I hope you can still see a little." Nora gestured toward Ian who held the cane in one hand. "I need you to test some stuff on this cane and let me know if it's blood. Can you do that?"

"Sure, that wouldn't be hard," Jen said, gesturing for them to follow her to a long black lab table near her desk. The whole room was full of identical tables, but this one held a microscope and a variety of tubes, jars, and small boxes. She held out her hand for the cane, and Ian handed it over.

She peered at the dark stains on the head of the cane. "Looks like it could be blood." She scraped some off with the tip of a lab scalpel, and then scraped it onto a test tube. She searched in one of several boxes until she found a small stopper-topped tube. As she worked, she talked, "It's basic chemistry. I'm testing for hemoglobin by the formation of crystals in chemical reaction. Blood has loads of iron in the hemoglobin and that reacts with pyridine to produce lovely red feathery crystals of pyridine ferroprotoporphyrin."

"Much as I love a good chemistry lesson," Nora said, "I mostly just want to know if it's blood."

Jen looked at her and shook her head as if deeply saddened by her friend's lack of interest in the science behind what she was doing. "It's blood," she said.

"Human?" Nora asked.

"Now that's a different test and not one I'm set up here to do. We don't do anything quite that complex in high school biology." She looked closer at the head of the cane. "There's a good bit of sample here. Let me scrape some more off and take it home where I have more reagents. I can call you as soon as I know. Would that be OK?"

"Sounds great," Nora said.

"So, is this for some newspaper story?" Jen asked.

"Could be," Nora said. "You haven't heard anything weird about Fuller's Island lately, have you?"

Jen looked surprised. "Actually I have. I heard a couple of kids talking about it the other day. They'd gone over a couple weeks ago and said they had heard a pack of dogs on the island. Scared them half to death, apparently. I thought maybe they had imagined it since that island is seriously creepy."

"I saw a video online," Annie said. "It was supposedly taken on the island, and it definitely sounded like there were dogs on the island."

"But we saw no sign of dogs this morning," Ian said.

"Dogs that appear and disappear?" Nora said. "I'm liking this story more every minute."

"You'll have to tell me how it turns out," Jen said. "I'll call you for sure after I run the test. I need to get home now and grade a pile of tests. That should depress me."

"Be brave," Nora said, thumping her friend lightly on

the back. "I'll wait for your call." She headed out into the hall with Ian and Annie, leaving Jen behind to stuff papers into her briefcase.

"So where to now, Nancy Drew?" Nora asked Annie. Then she turned to grin at Ian. "Which I suppose makes you Ned Nickerson?"

"I'm afraid I didn't read those books as a boy," Ian said.

"Ah, so more likely you're Frank Hardy," Nora said. "Still, what shall we sleuth next?"

"We've run out of ideas until we get on the island to-morrow," Ian said.

"In that case, drop me at the office," Nora told them. "I've got some other newspaper work to finish up before I head home."

"That sounds good," Ian said.

As they drove back to the office, Annie asked for a suggestion of where they might pick up some supper. "I'd like to bring something back for everyone besides pizza."

"The Chinese restaurant across the street here is really good," Nora said. "I think it's the Golden Dragon right now. It's changed owners three times since I moved back to town, but it's got the right folks now. The food is delicious."

They pulled into the parking lot for the newspaper. Ian and Annie got out of the car to walk Nora to the newspaper door. "An escort?" Nora asked.

"I've learned to be careful once the women around me start kicking hornets' nests," Ian told her. "It's best to keep an eye on them."

"I promise to be careful," Nora said.

Once she was safely inside, Ian and Annie crossed

the near empty street and walked into the small Chinese restaurant. From the tiny scattering of small closely grouped tables, it was clear the place did mostly a take-out business. They walked to the counter and stared up at the picture menu mounted close to the ceiling. The restaurant appeared to offer the same packed menu of items common to Chinese restaurants everywhere.

Ian ordered a little of a lot of different things so he'd be sure to have something everyone would like. The young Chinese girl who took their order spoke clear crisp English, but then called out to the people in the kitchen in Chinese. The flurry of activity following the girl's words was fascinating to watch, and they got all their food with amazing speed.

Loaded up with bags and cartons, Annie and Ian headed back out into the cooling evening. "The smell of all this is making my stomach growl," Annie complained. "I can't promise all the egg rolls are going to make it back to the inn."

Ian laughed. He turned his head at an odd scraping sound coming from the narrow alley between the Chinese restaurant and a cluster of shops next to it. Something about the sound made him pause, reaching out for Annie even as he peered toward the gloom of the alley. He realized he couldn't quite reach her as Annie stepped into the street. Ian sprinted toward Annie as a small car rocketed out of the alley straight at them.

Dropping the bags he was holding, Ian grabbed Annie, using his momentum to carry her along as he dove for a high concrete planter that ran parallel to the road. They made it into the planter as the car scraped along the concrete side and ran over most of their dinner bags.

Ian sat up, gently pulling Annie with him. "Are you OK?"

Annie nodded, panting slightly with alarm. "Maybe some bruises." She looked at Ian with wide eyes. "That didn't really feel like an accident."

"No," Ian said. "I think we've finally kicked the nest enough to bring out the hornets."

— 16 —

*Father's plan was a simple one. We would set up a camp
some distance from the closest outbuilding of my great-
grandfather's mansion. We would spend the night in tents,
draped in mosquito netting like explorers of the dark conti-
nent. In the morning, our fears would be shown as the silly
imaginings they were, and we would be free of them forever. It
was a simple plan and should have been a good one. Everyone
knows there is no such things as curses or ghosts—two-legged
or four. It was a simple plan—and very simply wrong.*

—Steven Fuller, 1925

Though Annie had lost a lot of her appetite in the near
accident, they returned to the restaurant to replace the
food scattered all over the parking lot. The girl from behind
the counter greeted them at the door as the rest of her family chattered rapidly behind her.

"Are you all right?" she asked.

"We're fine," Annie said. "Though that driver was certainly a little reckless. Did you happen to recognize the car?"

"No, I'm sorry," the girl said. "I don't pay much attention to cars. I don't drive." She turned and spoke to the rest
of the people in rapid Chinese. Several shook their heads
as they turned to file back toward the kitchen now that the
show was over.

One younger man paused at the kitchen doorway and turned to Annie and Ian. "I don't know who drives the car," he said, his English clear but slightly accented. "But I think I've seen it around. It's not the usual kind of car for around here. Expensive, you know?"

Ian nodded. "Thanks for the help."

The young man nodded. "I'm glad you weren't hurt."

He walked on into the kitchen, and Ian made the same food order as before. Again, the food was delivered quickly. This time, Ian insisted that Annie stay inside the restaurant with the food while he fetched the car. "I really don't want to buy it all again," he said when he saw her preparing to protest against his protectiveness.

"Fine," she said. "I'll wait." Annie was beginning to feel a little stiff and sore from the flying tackle into the planter. She suspected a long hot bath was in her future.

Annie didn't end up dipping into the egg rolls on the way back to the inn, though the knots in her stomach from the near miss were beginning to loosen by the time they arrived. They found Mary Beth, Stella, and Charles in the inn's dining room sipping tea with the double dining-room doors thrown open.

"You're back," Mary Beth said, hopping up. "And you brought presents!"

"Dinner," Annie said, holding up a bag. "And it smells wonderful."

"Excellent," Charles said. "We can eat it here. And you can tell us all about your afternoon of sleuthing. I have tried very hard to get more information from my sister, but she has turned into a veritable clam. A very grumpy clam at that. I was also not able to find a boat for us. I don't seem to have been of much use at all."

"Thanks for trying," Annie said.

Ian and Annie began unloading the bags onto the table. "I totally forgot about drinks," Ian said. "It's a good thing you have tea."

"I'm growing rather fond of Southern sweet tea," Stella said. "Though I suspect it isn't good for me."

Charles placed a hand over one of Stella's. "I hope that isn't the only Southern thing you're growing fond of."

Stella deftly slipped her hand free. "I suspect it isn't the only Southern thing that wouldn't be at all good for me."

Charles chuckled. "Living dangerously makes everything more fun, my dear."

"If you two are done," Mary Beth said, turning pointedly to Annie and Ian, "I want to hear about the sleuthing. And I'd like to know why your clothes look like you and Ian were rolling around in the bushes."

"We were," Ian said.

Mary Beth raised her eyebrows nearly to the top of her head.

"Not like that," Annie said. "Someone tried to run us over."

"Oh! An attempt on your lives!" Charles exclaimed. "How exciting! I feel like I've come home to star in a crime drama."

"Are you hurt?" Stella asked after giving Charles a reproving look.

"Only my dignity," Annie said. "But we should really

tell you about everything in order." She went through their visit to the boat rental and what Bob Maynard had said about Ellie.

"I don't believe that for a second," Mary Beth said fiercely.

"Neither did I," Annie admitted. "I just hope Ellie is OK where she is. With everything that's happened, this whole situation just looks worse and worse."

Ian gently took her hand and squeezed it. Then he told the others about their visit to the school, and the discovery that Jim's cane definitely had blood on it. "But we don't know that it's Jim's blood," Ian said. "At this point, we don't even know that it's human blood. So it's too soon to panic."

"Too late," Mary Beth said. "I'm feeling a little panicky about this whole thing, especially after someone tried to run you and Annie over. Did you call the police?"

"And tell them what?" Ian asked. "A small dark car driven by no one we could see almost hit us? Judging by our last visit to the police department, the chief is going to mark us down as hysterical tourists making a big thing out of a near accident."

"It didn't sound accidental," Mary Beth said.

"It wasn't," Ian agreed. "But that doesn't mean we'll convince the chief."

"Especially if he's in on this conspiracy," Stella said.

"Oh, I doubt the police chief is trying to cover up something criminal," Charles said, shaking his head.

"Would you have believed your sister was?" Stella asked.

Charles didn't answer, but Annie could tell the question hit home.

"Look—we have a plan for the moment," Ian said. "We should hear back about the blood in the morning, and we'll be going back out to the island with Nora."

Charles looked up in sharp surprise. "You found a boat?"

"Yes, Nora found it," Annie said.

"How unexpected," Charles said.

"Maybe you should call Nora," Mary Beth said worriedly. "To make sure no unfortunate car accident happened to her too."

Annie felt a pang of alarm, and she stepped away from the group to make the call. The newspaperwoman answered on the first ring and listened with concern to Annie's description of the near accident. "Nothing like that has happened to me," Nora said. "But I'll be careful. Look, I heard back from Jen. The blood is human, but that doesn't mean it belongs to either of your friends. From your description, I could easily believe your friend Jim walloped someone while defending himself."

"I can easily picture that too," Annie said, grateful for Nora's effort to make her feel better. "Thanks for everything you're doing to help. I just wanted to check on you, so I'll let you have the rest of the evening in peace. We'll see you in the morning."

"I'm looking forward to it," Nora said.

Shortly after Annie hung up the phone, she told her friends she was desperate for a hot bath and a quiet evening in her room. "I think my brain needs to think about something besides mystery."

"You should call LeeAnn," Mary Beth said. "Stories about the twins should take your mind off worry for a while."

It turned out Mary Beth was right. Annie's phone call to Texas was timed perfectly to catch the twins right after their bath time, and they were full of stories for their grandmother. They'd decided on their talent-show acts. John was going to do magic along with his singing assistant. Annie laughed as Joanna demonstrated her magical songs.

By the time Annie got off the phone, she felt much lighter—the cheerful children had lifted some of the weight that had settled on her shoulders. Annie scooped up a paperback book and carried it into the bathroom. She soaked in a hot bath and read, occasionally adding a little more hot water as the tub cooled. Finally, she felt almost limp from relaxation, so she finished her nighttime preparations, slipped into bed and quickly fell asleep.

Her dreams, however, pulled her back into the mystery, and she found herself running down the streets of Preacher's Reach. Some of the time she was chased by a small dark car, and sometimes her pursuer was a pack of dogs. Finally she turned a corner in the town and found her way blocked by a brick wall. She turned, her back against the wall, as the first dog leapt at her.

Annie woke with a gasp, sitting bolt upright. Faint morning light shone through the windows, telling Annie that dawn was near. She'd forgotten to set her alarm for an early start, but the nightmare had worked better than any alarm at snapping her awake.

She swung her legs out of bed and waited a moment for her heart to stop pounding. Then she dressed for another visit to the swampy island. As she debated which pair of shoes to ruin, she wondered if there was a discount shoe store in Preacher's Reach. She certainly didn't like the idea of driving back to Stony Point in shoes that stunk of swamp.

Just as she finished, she heard a light tap at the door and opened it to find Ian. He smiled warmly at her. "Did you sleep?" he asked.

She nodded. "Though my dreams featured cars and dogs a little too much."

Ian rested his hands on Annie's shoulders. "I won't let anything hurt you," he said.

Annie smiled and answered softly, "I know."

Ian leaned closer to Annie, and she had a startled moment of wondering if he was going to whisper to her or kiss her. Then a voice spoke from the hallway. "Good," Stella said. "You're both ready. The rest of us are as well."

Ian sighed and took his hands away from Annie's shoulders. He turned to Stella slowly. "Is Mary Beth downstairs?"

"Yes," Stella said. "And Charles as well. I offered to come up and check on your progress."

"Well, we're ready," Annie said as she eased out of the room around Ian. "Let's go."

They walked together down the lovely maple staircase. Stella lead the way into the dining room where Charles and Mary Beth sat sipping coffee.

"I suppose you two should eat something," Stella said reluctantly.

"Are you planning to go to the island?" Annie asked in surprise. "I thought you preferred to be our mainland backup."

"I talked her into it," Charles said. "I want to come with you, and I thought perhaps having some extra eyes for the search would be good."

"The terrain is very uneven," Ian said hesitantly.

"I can handle it," Charles said. "And if Stella grows tired, I'll watch over her while we sit and rest."

Annie smiled slightly at the cool look Stella offered him. Annie and Ian ate a quick breakfast as their friends chatted. Now and then Mrs. Ayers passed through the room and scowled at them. Charles always made a point to beam back at her with his wide smile.

"You shouldn't tease your sister," Stella scolded.

"That's what sisters are for," Charles said, giving Mrs. Ayers a cheery little finger wave that made her scowl so deep her eyes nearly disappeared.

"I'm not certain how big the boat we're borrowing is," Ian said. "It may not hold all of us."

"In that case, I'll wait on the shore with Stella," Charles said, casting calf eyes at Stella and receiving a frown in return.

"I'd like to go," Mary Beth said. "But if there's no room, I'll stay on shore and keep Stella from throwing Charles into the water."

"I would hardly resort to violence," Stella said.

Annie actually suspected that Stella rather enjoyed the attention from the handsome Southerner, though she doubted her friend would *ever* admit it. Charles was so over the top and theatrical—all the things Stella wasn't.

As Annie sipped her coffee, her cellphone began to buzz in her purse. After a moment of rooting around, she fished it out and found that Nora was calling.

"I'm ready to go," Nora said. "Are you guys set? I can give you directions to my house, and you can meet me there."

"Sounds good," Annie said. She pulled a pen from her

purse and wrote the directions on a receipt she found in her wallet. Finally, she told Nora they'd be leaving right away from the inn. After the call, they all headed for the car, eager to begin the hunt.

As they pulled out of the inn parking lot, Annie saw Mrs. Ayers standing on the porch watching them, her arms crossed over her chest.

Annie read the directions to Ian as he drove, and they found Nora sitting on the front steps of a small house trailer sipping coffee. The trailer sat on the wide side yard of a weathered cottage.

As they piled out of the SUV, Nora walked toward them with a smile. "Looks like we've got quite a search party," she said.

Annie introduced her around, ending with, "And I think you know Charles Bonneau."

"Since I was in diapers," Nora said with a grin. "Does Mom know you're in town?"

"No!" Charles cast an alarmed glance toward the small cottage. "I would prefer it remained so."

Nora laughed. "I'm sure she's not still mad at you."

Charles looked less sure, and Stella's face lit up with curiosity. "Mad about what?"

"Charles made some unfortunate remarks about people who believe in the paranormal at a lecture Mom dragged him to," Nora said.

Charles rolled his eyes. "That ridiculous speaker showed off a pile of blurry, splotchy photos and played scratchy sound recordings. It was the silliest thing I've ever been subjected to."

"You know Mom is crazy for that stuff," Nora said.

"I didn't know she was past all reason," Charles grumbled.

"Guess you know now!" Nora laughed and turned to Ian. "I'm ready. I was going to offer my car, but we wouldn't all fit, so I guess you're driving."

"I actually prefer it," Ian said.

Nora took the "shotgun" seat since she needed to help navigate to where they would pick up the boat. Annie took the rear seat beside Mary Beth. As they drove, Annie enjoyed watching Charles trying to charm Stella. From Mary Beth's almost constant grin, Annie suspected the charming Southerner would be the topic of a lengthy story to the Hook and Needle Club when they got home.

The drive lasted nearly an hour. Finally, they pulled up in front of a lovely A-frame house with a boat launch in the backyard. A big man in jeans and a flannel shirt with the sleeves torn out sat on a low deck attached to the house.

"Andrew!" Nora shouted. "Where did you get that shirt, and how did you keep Jen from throwing it out?"

"I hide it when she's around," he said, grinning. White teeth shone from behind the thick beard the man wore. "You're right on time. Wow, you do have a crew!"

Nora introduced everyone, and Andrew nodded pleasantly. "I hate to rain on your parade, Nora, but I think you've got too many people."

"Oh please," Nora said. "That boat of yours is a beast. I know we'd all fit."

"It's not fitting that's going to be the problem," Andrew said. "It's weight. My boat has a pretty shallow draft. You have to around here because the depth is all over the place offshore. But if you put enough weight in the boat, you run the risk of bottoming out, especially around Fuller's Island. I don't think you'd get close enough to get out of the boat. Not unless you're going to tow a rowboat and anchor offshore."

Nora seemed to think about that. "Do you have a rowboat?"

"Sure," he said. "But you better keep my boat off the rocks."

"Scout's honor," Nora said.

Andrew led them to the boat and helped hitch a long rowboat to the back of the bigger craft. Annie didn't have a lot of experience with boats, but the difference between the gleaming white boat in front of her and Ellie's ragged craft were astonishing. The front of the boat curved up almost like a slipper from an *Arabian Nights* tale.

Everyone climbed aboard and found a place to sit. Ian joined Nora in casting off, and then followed her to the pilot's seat. Though Nora drove, she smiled and promised Ian that he could pilot on the way back.

They cruised lightly over the water, and Annie found the ride amazingly smooth. She glanced over at Stella, who sat with Charles's arm around her. Stella looked tense and a little pale, but Annie couldn't tell if the speed of the boat made her nervous or the arm of the man beside her.

For most of the ride, nothing looked familiar to Annie. The coastal shore was mostly narrow beach with a few small docks that appeared to be private for the most part.

"Is that the island?" Mary Beth asked, touching Annie's

arm. Annie turned in the direction Mary Beth pointed and spotted an overgrown island.

"I think it might be. It's overgrown enough," Annie said. "I don't know how many islands are out here."

She knew it must be the place when Nora slowed the boat to a stop. "OK, the rest of the way is going to be a little harder work," Nora called. "I think someone should stay with Andrew's boat. I hate to be paranoid, but I like the idea of it being here when we get back."

"I'll stay," Stella said. "I don't think I could scramble into and out of a rowboat very easily."

"And I'll keep Stella company," Charles offered with a smile.

Ian helped Nora haul the rowboat closer. Nora hopped in and helped Annie over and then Mary Beth. Finally, Ian climbed in, and they were ready to go.

"We should have an expected time for your return," Stella called to them. "So we know when to go find help if we need it."

"Well, you said you searched the main buildings," Nora said. "But there are some smaller outbuildings on the other side of the island. With hiking over to check on them and searching, we probably need five hours."

"Why didn't we simply take the boat to that side?" Stella asked.

"No place to land safely," Nora said. "Or none that I know of. We'll see you both in about five hours."

"I'm sure we'll find some way to pass the time," Charles said as he helped cast off the rowboat.

Ian took up the oars at his seat and began rowing briskly

toward the island. Nora settled into the second set of oars and quickly matched Ian's rhythm. Annie and Mary Beth sat at either end of the boat and kept their eyes on the approaching coastline.

"When we came over the first time, we left the boat in a hidden cove," Annie said.

"I know where that is," Nora said, her voice slightly breathy from the rowing. "But we're not near there. We can beach instead. This is about the only really clear easy beach on the island."

Soon enough, they drew close to the beach and the small boat bottomed out. "OK, everyone out, and we tow the boat to shore."

The shallow water was shockingly cold as it soaked Annie's sneakers instantly and wicked up the legs of her dark cotton pants. Annie grabbed the side of the boat and pulled it toward shore. With all four of them pulling, they beached the boat easily, dragging it well past the tide line.

"The closest path to the buildings I mentioned is this way," Nora said, wading through the soft, dry sand until she reached the firmer ground that signaled the edge of the undergrowth.

Everyone followed her, and they walked in silence through the thickening woods. This time the path was a bit clearer, and Annie wondered if this was the way visiting teens normally went. Certainly the path had seen more use than the one Ellie had taken them on.

They reached a spot where the path divided, and Nora took the left way. "This one hugs the coast," she said. "So it'll take us to the buildings I mentioned. The other path is a more direct way to cross the island, but we'd have to do some bushwhacking as it doesn't go all the way to the coast on the other side."

"I think I'd prefer no bushwhacking," Ian said. "We're not equipped for it."

The thick humidity of the island soon had Annie feeling like a damp rag. The cuffs of Annie's pants were soaked with salt, and they rubbed her shins like sandpaper. Finally, Annie paused to roll up her pant legs to give her skin a break.

Time passed with no sound except the buzz of insects everywhere and the occasional rustling burst when they disturbed a bird or other creature in the brush around them. Annie constantly waved away gnats that seemed determined to fly into her eyes.

Annie began to walk more quickly, hoping to outrun the pesky gnats, and she soon passed Mary Beth and Ian. She fell in step behind Nora but definitely found that she had not outrun the annoying insects.

Suddenly, Nora stopped in front of her so quickly that Annie nearly ran into her. "Do you hear that?" Nora asked.

Annie shook her head, but they all stopped and listened. Annie heard something far in the distance. The sound was mournful and long. "That sounded like a howl," Mary Beth said.

"It's so far away," Ian said. "Could have been mechanical. A foghorn maybe?"

"I don't know," Nora said. "It sounded like a dog to me."

"We should be able to tell more as we get closer," Ian said.

The group picked up their pace. The unusual sound had

lightened everyone's sagging spirits. If they could find the mysterious dogs of the island, maybe they could find out what happened to Jim and Alice.

~ 17 ~

The sound of the dogs awoke us. First, the lone baying of a distant hound could be heard. The sound frightened me and I shrieked. Father told me the sound had come from the mainland, carried on the wind. I might have believed him except for the further howls and snarls that came ever closer. Father had brought a pistol, and he held it in an iron grip as he towed me through the dark woods toward the main house. I knew if we reached the house and the light before the dogs, we would live. If we did not ... we would die.

—Steven Fuller, 1925

The intermittent sound of the dogs stayed faint for what seemed to be another hour of walking, but finally it became clear enough to be certain. Nora had picked up her pace until Annie was huffing to keep up.

They raced along the trail for a while, and then slowed down, finally coming to a stop. "I don't hear them anymore," Nora said, panting.

"Nor do I," Ian said. "Do you know of anything close to here where someone might keep dogs?"

Nora looked around. "We're close to a small outbuilding," she answered tentatively. "I've never been in it, though I've seen it. I don't know how many dogs someone could cram in it."

"Let's check and see," Ian said.

"We need to go that way," Nora said, pointing into the underbrush. "We should meet another trail eventually, but it'll be rough going for a while. I remember the outbuilding being on high ground and more inland."

Nora waded off into the brush and Ian followed, stomping down as much brush as he could to make the way easier for Annie and Mary Beth. Even so, Annie had to concentrate to avoid stumbling, and once she barely caught Mary Beth when she tripped and nearly hit the ground. They definitely weren't moving very fast.

"I wonder why we don't hear the dogs anymore," Mary Beth said.

"Maybe we're heading away from them?" Annie asked, though the sounds she'd heard earlier certainly seemed to come from this direction.

"Acoustics can be funny on an island with so much undergrowth and different levels of terrain," Ian said as he stomped through the brush. "I think we need to keep going and see this building. If nothing comes of it, we can always retrace our steps."

Annie looked around at the broken brush, it certainly wouldn't be hard to see where they'd come from.

Finally, the heavy brush ended and they were back on a trail. As they walked along the smoother ground, they each picked sticks and burrs out of their clothes and hair. Annie felt some bit of stick down the front of her shirt and reached in to pull it out. It came out wiggling with legs and antenna. She shrieked and tossed the bug into the brush.

Ian spun and rushed back to her. "Are you OK?"

"Yeah, sorry," she said, her face burning with embarrassment. "I had some kind of cockroach in my shirt. I guess I overreacted a little."

Ian smiled at her and picked a leaf out of her hair. "I don't know, they have big cockroaches down here. I might have screamed a little myself."

"Hey, listen," Nora said. "Sounds like Annie woke them up again."

Everyone fell quiet, and then they heard it—barking. The sound was muffled but clearly seemed to come from up ahead. They picked up the pace, trotting up the trail as quickly as they dared. Finally, they spotted signs of a building through the brush before breaking into the clearing where a low cinder-block building squatted.

The building looked much more recently built than anything Ian and Annie had seen on their previous visit. It was fairly small—as Nora had said—but the closer they got, the more clearly they could hear the dogs. Still, the sound of barking was weirdly muffled. It was as if it came from inside the building, but still far away. Annie wondered if the lack of windows in the building could be what muffled the sound so much.

They reached the strong metal door and found it firmly locked. "Looks like this is as far as we go," Ian said.

"Such little faith," Nora said. She pulled a small zippered pouch from the rucksack she carried. Annie leaned closer to see as Nora unzipped the pouch. The contents looked almost like dental tools to Annie.

"Lock picks?" Ian said incredulously. "You can pick locks?"

"I hung out with some wild boys during my misspent

youth," Nora said. Then she added. "Plus, I sorta wanted to be a detective. Picking locks seemed like a useful detective skill."

She bent and concentrated on the lock, poking and twisting tools in it. Annie wondered idly if Nora could teach her to do that. With all the trouble she got into regularly with her mysteries, being able to unlock a door might be useful.

Nora hooted softly with triumph as she pulled the door open. The inside of the building was dark as pitch. Everyone stepped back in case the dogs they heard cared to rush out, but nothing inside moved. They could still hear the dogs, but the sound continued to be muffled.

"That's just weird," Nora said.

They slipped inside in a tight single-file line, with Ian stepping into the lead. It seemed as if the cinder blocks trapped all the heat and moisture of the island. Annie felt as if she were instantly drenched in sweat, and she wiped her face with her hand.

"Oh, wait," Nora said once they were totally engulfed by the darkness. "I'm such an idiot! I've got a flashlight." They heard the sound of her rummaging through her rucksack. "Here it is."

As she snapped on the light, someone spoke from behind them. "Don't move." They all moved. They spun to face the source of the sound, and the man groaned, "You people don't follow directions worth anything!"

"Who are you?" Ian demanded.

The man they faced didn't look at all familiar. He was

broad-shouldered with thick muscles straining against the fabric of his T-shirt. His head was shaved down to stubble, and he sported a large adhesive bandage on his forehead. In his right hand, he held a very scary gun.

"I've got the gun," the man said. "I make the demands, so put your hands up!"

Annie and her friends raised their hands.

"Do you know this guy?" Ian asked, looking at Nora.

She shook her head. "He's not local."

"Did I ask you people to chat?" The man gestured with his gun. "We're heading downstairs. Turn around. The stairs are just ahead of you. Find them and get moving."

"Downstairs?" Annie turned and looked around, but most of the room was too dark to see. Nora's flashlight beam swung around, finally hitting a low wall in the middle of the room. They walked toward it and soon saw it ran alongside the stairs the man mentioned.

Nora led the way down the stairs, and the others followed. Ian dropped back to the rear so he was closest to the man with the gun. Annie didn't like that at all and hoped Ian didn't feel like he had to risk himself to save them.

At the bottom of the stairs, they met another heavy metal door. "Bang on it with your flashlight," the gunman said.

Nora rapped on it with the flashlight, and the door swung open. Bright light flooded them, making them all blink, suddenly light-blinded.

They stumbled into a huge room. The temperature was a radical drop from the sweltering air above. Annie blinked, looking around through slitted eyes. The walls of the underground room looked damp, reminding Annie that a basement on an island couldn't possibly be a good idea.

From behind the door, a skinny man with a bulging Adam's apple and shaggy comb-over watched them nervously. "Did you have to bring them down here, Oscar?" he asked.

"Seemed smarter than shooting them upstairs and leaving pools of blood," the muscled gunman said.

Nora turned to look at the skinny man and groaned, "Leroy, really? You're mixed up in this?"

"Shut up," the gunman said, giving Nora a shove.

Annie glanced around the room, and then she gasped. "Alice!" she said. "Jim!"

Jim and Alice stood in a huge metal cage near the far back wall. They were dirty but seemed unharmed as they pressed against the bars. "Oh, Annie," Alice said. "I'm so sorry."

"You'll have plenty of time for your reunion," the gunman said. "I'll just let y'all reconnect." He gestured with his gun for the group to walk toward the big cage.

They were basically walking down a long aisle. On either side, big dog cages stacked two high filled most of the rest of the room. In each cage, at least one dog stared avidly at them. In a couple cages, puppies pressed against the bars of the cage with a larger dog looming over them.

The dogs were big, muscular, and almost universally black. They had short hair, to the point of looking almost hairless, and big heads with massive jaws. Small ears hugged their heads, and they had no tails at all.

When they reached the huge cage that held Jim and Alice, the gunman waved them back away from the door.

"All the way to the wall, old man," the gunman said. "You don't want to get frisky again. Someone could get shot. Open the door, Leroy."

"Not me," the nervous man said. "I'm not getting near any of them. Let the girl do it."

"Hey, little princess!" the gunman yelled. "Get out here!"

That's when Annie got the biggest shock of all. Ellie came up from behind them and walked past quickly before shoving a key into the cage door. She turned it and pulled the door open. She didn't make eye contact with anyone as she obeyed the gunman.

"OK, Scooby Doo gang—into the cage," the man said. "You first, mister. I don't want you hanging back and looking for trouble."

Ian glared at the man but walked into the cage. Annie, Mary Beth, and Nora followed. Ellie locked the door behind them. "Ellie," Annie called, and the girl jumped, her eyes darting to Annie. "Are you OK?"

"No fraternizing with the prisoners," the gunman said. He grabbed Ellie by the arm and hauled her across the room. Leroy followed them, tugging nervously at his shirt collar. From the cage, Annie could see that the area closer to the stairs had been set up to store dog food and supplies. The gunman slung an arm around Ellie, and they walked through another door in the wall near the stairs.

Once the door closed, Annie turned and engulfed Alice in a hug. "I'm so glad to see you," Annie said as she blinked back tears. "The longer we were here, the more I wondered if I'd ever see you again."

"Me too," Alice said.

"I know the thought crossed my mind once or twice," Jim said from where he leaned against the far wall.

"What is going on here?" Ian said.

Jim gestured in an expansive sweep at the rows of cages. "Dogs," he said. "They're breeding some kind of super fighting dog."

"Fighting dog?" Annie said, her voice hushed as she looked at the rows of cages.

"Dogfights are big money," Nora said, shaking her head sadly. "Dogs ripping each other apart while monsters bet on them."

"That's horrible," Annie said.

"But why here?" Ian asked.

Jim shrugged. "The legendary curse, I imagine. If trespassers happen to hear dogs on the island, they're blown off as over-imaginative. This place is private, off the beaten path. A pretty good lair really."

Alice turned toward Nora. "Hi, I'm Alice MacFarlane. This is my friend Jim Parker. And you are?"

"Nora Harlow," Nora said. "Ace reporter. Or girl most likely to get captured by evil villains. It depends on who you ask."

"How many people are involved in this?" Ian asked. "Other than Oscar, Leroy, and Ellie."

"Ellie is a recent addition," Alice said. "She's gone along with everything since she got here, but she did pass me a note."

Alice fished it out of her jeans and held it out. The paper was creased and dirty, but the block printing was exactly like the note they'd gotten at the pizza parlor. It said: "Your friends are coming."

"We'd hoped for more of a cavalry kind of entrance from you guys," Jim said dryly, "and less of a fellow prisoner approach."

Ian sighed. "Me too."

"Anyway," Jim said, "Oscar is the one who grabbed us from the mansion after we found one of the dogs. Leroy seems to be more in charge of covering things up."

"Leroy is the police officer that Chief Harper mentioned?" Annie asked.

Nora nodded. "I knew Leroy was lazy, but I didn't expect him to be tied up in this."

"You said you found one of the dogs?" Ian asked, turning back to Jim.

"Yeah, apparently they get away now and then," Jim said. "Though they can't get far. They can't swim—too much muscle."

"They're not bad dogs," Alice said. "The one we found was sweet, just really big and really hungry."

"Anyway, it seems the dogfighters were just hoping I'd take my photos and go away none the wiser," Jim said. "Apparently the plan was to just lie low, but that changed when we found the dog and acted like we were going to take it with us to the mainland. Then Oscar came out of nowhere ... ."

"And you hit him with your cane," Ian said, smiling. "We found it. And I'm glad to know the blood wasn't yours."

Jim grinned back. "I really don't like being told what to do."

"So it's just the two men and Ellie?" Annie asked.

Alice shook her head. "At first we thought it was just the one man. We nearly got away, until Leroy caught up to us at the cove."

"Well, we now know why Leroy couldn't find y'all in his searches," Nora said.

"Chief Harper said Leroy was out of town on a family emergency," Ian said.

"He's been here nearly full-time since they grabbed us," Jim said. "Oscar left for a while with some of the dogs, but he came back yesterday with Ellie."

"Do they ever let you out of the cage?" Ian asked.

"There's a bathroom in there," Alice said, pointing toward the back wall with the door. "And when one of them is feeling generous, we get to go there. Otherwise ... ." She gestured toward a pail in the corner of the room.

"Oh, great!" Mary Beth said.

"I'm not planning to be here long," Ian said. "Charles Bonneau and Stella are in the boat waiting for us."

"Bonneau? Who's he?" Alice asked.

"He's the brother of the Ayers woman at the inn," Ian explained.

"She wasn't one of our biggest fans."

"We noticed," Annie said. "We were lied to by a lot of people in Preacher's Reach about you two. Have you seen anyone else from the town out here?"

Alice shook her head. "But I heard the muscled guy tell Ellie that he thought her uncle would find it much easier to stick with the program with Ellie on the island."

"So this guy could be controlling people by threats," Ian said. "But why would a whole town be afraid of one man?"

"Because dogfight rings are never one man," Nora said. "One may be all we're seeing, but power and money are wrapped up in this somehow."

"Do you know what they're planning to do with us?" Mary Beth asked.

"They don't seem to have reached an agreement," Jim said. "Oscar was in favor of killing us. I think he's holding a grudge for the smack in the head. But Leroy doesn't like the idea of being involved in murder. Apparently they're waiting to hear from a more important voice in the food chain."

"I wouldn't bet too highly on a vote in our favor," Nora said.

"I'm still counting on Stella and Charles," Annie said.

"Certainly, the disappearance of six people will be a little harder to cover up than the disappearance of two," Ian said. "Too many people know exactly where we are and why we're here."

Within the hour, Ellie and the gunman came out of the back room. Ellie carried sacks of food that she passed through the bars of the cage while the man watched, his gun still in his hand.

"Ellie," Annie said softly. "Are you OK?"

The girl nodded slightly as she shoved a bottle of water into Annie's hand.

Just as she passed the last bottle, they heard the sound of a distant explosion, followed by another. The second sounded closer and Annie could feel vibration in the floor under her feet.

"What the ...?" the gunman turned sharply toward the

stairs, and then back to Ellie. "You come with me." He hauled the girl across the room and up the stairs.

"Could that be our rescue?" Nora asked.

"With explosions?" Alice said. "Isn't that a little to dramatic to be Stella?"

"I don't know what it was," Ian said, turning to Nora, "but this might be a good time to try your lock-picking skills again."

"The picks are in my rucksack," Nora said, pointing to a spot just out of reach where the gunman had tossed it.

"That I should be able to help you with," Jim said. Leaning heavily on the back wall, he hauled his pant leg up and quickly unstrapped one of his prosthetic legs. Holding it up, he grinned. "Instant reach extender. Just don't lose it. I'm planning to use it to get out of here."

Ian took the prosthetic and knelt down at the bars closest to the sack. He carefully pushed the prosthetic through the bars, snagging the rucksack strap with the foot of the prosthetic and hauling it back into the cage.

"Good fishing, Ian," Jim said as Ian handed him back his leg.

"And thank you for the leg up—or should I say out?" Ian quipped.

Nora pulled out the lock-pick kit and went to work on the cage lock while Jim put his leg back on with Alice helping support him.

In the distance, they heard one more explosion just as Nora sprang the lock. They piled out of the cage, and Ian strode quickly toward the stairs. "Hold on," Alice said. "We need to let the dogs out."

"Are you sure that's a good idea?" Mary Beth asked, looking at the massive animals in the cages. "We don't need to fight bad guys and dogs."

"Let's do it this way," Jim said. "Walk to the cage, if the dog growls, leave it. If it seems friendly, let it out. The confusion can only help us. Plus, if the guys try to destroy the evidence once we're gone, it'll be a lot harder to manage if the evidence is running and howling all over the island."

"Good plan." Ian turned to the cage nearest to him and knelt in front of it. The dog inside wagged its whole rear end when Ian spoke to it.

Annie walked tentatively to the cage closest to her. She loved animals, but the dogs were so big. She knelt in front of the cage and spoke to the dog softly. It looked at her with its big dark eyes but didn't wag its tail like Ian's dog. "Should I let you out?" she whispered. The dog just stared.

Annie thought about the gunman coming back to destroy evidence. This dog could die if she left it. She carefully opened the door, stepping out of the way as she did. The dog walked out slowly before turning toward Annie. Annie tried to back up, but the cage was at her back. The dog delicately licked her hand, and then turned and raced for the stairs.

Annie nearly collapsed from relief. All around her, cages were being opened and dogs were rushing out. Without fail, they headed for the stairs. Clearly Annie and her friends weren't the only ones who didn't like captivity.

Finally, almost all of the cages were empty. The only cages they didn't dare open held females with puppies. The mother dogs snarled as soon as they got close to the cage. Alice didn't like leaving the animals behind, but they didn't have much choice. They couldn't fight bad guys and dogs at the same time.

With the dogs gone, the group moved toward the stairs. Since Jim still didn't have his cane, he leaned on Alice for support. Ian moved slowly up the stairs, well aware that the man with the gun could be waiting at the top. The upper room was dim but not as pitch dark as before. The gunman had left the outside door open in his haste to track down the explosions. The light from that door and the light from the downstairs room made the upper room passable.

"It's clear," Ian said behind him as he quickly cleared the stairs.

When everyone stood on the upper level, he moved to the door as cautiously as he'd climbed the stairs. He took a quick look out, but no gunshot rang out, so he stepped out into the clearing, motioning for the others to follow him.

"OK, Nora," Ian said. "From here it's up to you. Can you find us the shortest way to the boat?"

Nora nodded and they followed her across the clearing and onto a new path they hadn't walked before. They moved as quickly and quietly as they could until they heard rustling in the brush ahead. Everyone froze.

Time ticked by, Annie barely dared breathe, expecting the man with the gun to appear at any moment. Instead, Nora's friend Andrew charged through the brush ahead of them, halting with a yelp when he saw the group.

After the moment of shock, his face lit up. "Nora!" he said. "I found you."

"What are you doing here?" Nora asked.

"I brought him."

The voice came from behind Andrew. He stepped out of the way to reveal Stella, looking as out of place as possible in her neat beige suit and sensible shoes. "When you didn't return, I insisted upon going to the mainland for help," Stella said. "That's when Charles showed his true colors. He tried to force me out of the boat! I had to smack him on the head with some odd tool thing I found and pilot the boat back myself!"

"Where did the explosions come from?" Ian asked.

"Me," Andrew said. "I make fireworks. It's not my smartest hobby and not strictly legal, but it comes in handy when you need a big boom."

"Do you know where the man with the gun is?" Annie asked.

Andrew shook his head. "Probably near the main buildings where I had the fireworks set to blow."

"You blew up buildings?" Nora asked, eyes wide.

"No, of course not," Andrew said. "I blew up some of the rubble though."

"The gunman has Ellie," Annie said. "We need to get her."

"Ellie was with them," Mary Beth said.

"She's also just a kid," Jim said. "We can't leave without her."

Since Jim and Alice had to be the two most eager to get off Fuller's Island, Annie felt her heart warm with pride at her friend.

"So how do we find them?" Stella asked.

Suddenly the group jumped as gunshots rang out in the near distance. "Sounds like a clue to me," Andrew said. "Though I never thought I'd run toward gunfire."

"I don't think we all need to go," Ian said. "Andrew and I can check out the gunshots and try to get Ellie while the rest of you head for the boat."

"Yeah," Mary Beth said. "That's not going to work. We're all going to rescue Ellie." She gave Ian a slight push, and they all turned back to the path. They moved as carefully as possible.

"The clearing with the main buildings isn't far now," Nora whispered after a few minutes.

They slipped into the clearing, and Alice cried out softly. One of the large dogs lay on the ground ahead of them. She slipped out from under Jim's arm and ran to the dog, kneeling beside it. The dog raised its head and licked her hand. "It's been shot," Alice said.

"I guess we know why the guy was shooting," Ian said quietly. "I think we can sneak up on the bad guy easier with fewer people. Could I talk some of you into staying here?"

"I'll stay," Stella said.

"I'm with Red," Jim said. "Whatever she wants to do."

Alice looked up, blinking tears. "I'm going to stay with the dog."

"I'll stay too," Mary Beth said.

Nora pointed at Ian. "I'm with you. When we get out of here, I'm going to have the story of the century."

"I'm coming too," Annie said. "I've spent enough time wondering if my friends are all still alive. I don't want to stay behind and worry about you too."

Andrew took the lead just ahead of Ian since he had more experience on the island. Annie followed close behind them, and Nora stayed on Annie's heels. They walked carefully through the brush and debris as they approached the buildings. At any moment, Annie expected to hear another gunshot, but she forced one foot in front of the other.

Ian stopped and held up his hand. When everyone froze, they heard voices up ahead. Ian crept forward until they could see around the building. To their surprise, they saw the gunman facing Bob Maynard and Ellie. Maynard kept his eyes on the other man's gun, but he didn't back down.

"I just want Ellie," Maynard said. "I don't care about the dogs."

"I don't like it when townies get all mouthy with me," the gunman said. "I have enough trouble. Now if you don't want to carry a bullet home in your guts, then the girl needs to come with me."

Ellie started to step around her uncle, but the tall man put out an arm to block her way. "We're done doing what you say. There's too many people involved. This is coming out into the open, and I'm not going to be associated with anything that gets people killed."

"I have it under control," the gunman snarled.

Then Annie heard another snarl, this one deeper and much, much scarier. A huge black dog slammed into the gunman from behind. The gun fired as the man went down, and Annie heard Ellie scream.

The second the man hit the ground, Ian and Andrew were on him, pulling the gun away. The man tried to fight at first, but the dog stood directly over his face, growling and snapping until the man stopped thrashing. "Get that thing off me," he whispered.

"Funny," Ian said. "They seem to like everyone but you."

"Just get it off."

"No, I don't think so," Ian said. "But I do recommend you lay very, very still."

While the men were subduing the gunman, Annie ran toward Ellie. The girl was fussing over her uncle who stood with one hand clasped over his arm. Blood leaked from between his fingers, and he looked distinctly paler.

"How bad is it?" Annie asked.

"Hurts like you wouldn't believe," Maynard said. "But I don't think it's bad."

Nora began pulling bandages and tape from her knapsack. She alternated between clucking over the wound and scolding Maynard for ever going along with the dogfighters. "I know, I know," Maynard said. "I just didn't want to risk Ellie."

"How did that work out for you?" Nora snapped.

"You're right," Maynard said wearily. "I've been an idiot."

Annie turned back to where Ian and Andrew were tying the gunman's hands behind his back with strips torn from Andrew's shirt. "I'm going to miss that shirt," Andrew said mournfully, jerking the makeshift rope tighter.

As they talked, the rest of their friends filed into the clearing with the wounded dog limping along beside them. "Well, looks like you didn't need us to rescue you," Alice said.

The dog that had tackled the gunman trotted over to the other dog and began sniffing noses in a friendly way.

"Looks like we're ready to go," Jim said.

"But we're still missing a bad policeman," Annie said.

"Maybe we'll find him along the way," Ian said. With the dogs along, I don't think he'll sneak up on us." They reached the narrow path and began trooping along.

"I'm already dreaming of the long, hot bath waiting for me," Alice said.

"Once we find a different inn," Stella said with a sniff. "I doubt our accommodations at the Ayers's will be available once the chief arrests Mrs. Ayers and her ridiculous brother."

"Come on, Stella," Mary Beth said. "Didn't you find him at least a little charming?"

"I thought he was very charming," Stella said seriously. "That's one reason I didn't trust him. Men like him don't waste charm on women their own age—not without a reason."

"He could have just liked you," Annie said.

Stella smiled slightly. "If he did, I doubt he does now."

Suddenly, the group heard barking coming from up ahead. "Leroy, maybe?" Nora said.

Ian and Andrew took the lead with Bob Maynard watching the prisoner closely. They broke into a tiny clearing not far from the cove. The dogs were clustered around one of the twisted trees that dripped moss. The tree held Leroy, clinging to a branch. His pants were torn, and Annie could see a trickle of blood on his leg.

"Help!" Leroy shouted. "They tried to kill me."

"Good for them!" Alice called back.

It took the group a few minutes to coax the dogs away

from the tree. It helped that Nora had shoved a food bag from the cage into her knapsack. The dogs definitely preferred sandwiches over the taste of Leroy. The group brought the injured dog with them. They would take him to a veterinarian when they got back to the mainland.

Finally, the group and their prisoners reached the cove where Ellie had first taken them and where Bob Maynard had left his boat.

"What are we going to do about the rest of the dogs?" Alice asked. "Just leave them?"

"Once we let the authorities know they're here, someone will come out," Nora said.

"But will they be OK?" Alice asked.

Nora shrugged helplessly. "I don't know. They're nice dogs, but they were bred to be dangerous. I'm not sure what will happen to them."

Alice cast sad eyes back toward the jungle before following everyone into Maynard's boat. He gave them a lift out to where Andrew had dropped anchor.

Charles Bonneau sat tied up in Andrew's boat. "This has all been a misunderstanding," he insisted.

"No way are you getting out of this, Bonneau," the bound gunman said.

"You should be quiet until you talk to your lawyer, young man," Bonneau told him.

"Forget it," the bound gunman said. "The one thing I'm not planning to be is quiet."

"How could you be involved in dogfighting?" Stella asked. "That's vile!"

Charles Bonneau smiled his charming smile, but Annie

found it less appealing now. "There is nothing more thrilling than betting on a blood sport, my dear," he said.

"I'm not 'your dear,'" Stella snapped. Then she took a seat as far as possible from the two men and rode the rest of the way to the mainland in silence.

~ 18 ~

We never saw the dogs, not really. I have memories of eyes glowing in the darkness and dark shapes moving through the brush. I remember running and falling and being pulled to my feet by my father. I remember reaching the house with the stench of death chasing us. But I don't know how much was real and how much imagined. I wonder now. What would I find if I returned to the family island? What lurks in the darkness of the overgrown gardens and forgotten buildings? I wonder about these things and about how long it will be until curiosity drives me to the island again. And if it does, will I ever leave ... alive?

—Steven Fuller, 1925

It took a couple of days to tie up all the loose ends and track down all of Jim and Alice's belongings. Jim's cameras were still in the basement of the dog-breeding building when they led the police back to the lair. His car was hidden not far from Maynard's boat rental shop. Both Maynard and Chief Harper did a lot of apologizing.

They learned that Charles Bonneau was the one who thought Fuller's Island would be the perfect spot for breeding a new kind of fighting dog. When Annie heard the amounts of money involved, she was shocked and horrified. Apparently the amounts were enough to entice

Bonneau's sister over to the dark side with him.

They didn't find anyone else who knew exactly what was happening on Fuller's Island. Most of the people just kept quiet because Maynard asked them to, and his own involvement began and ended with being threatened.

"When I went out to find my boat," Maynard said, "that's when I met that goon Oscar. He had a gun and made it sound like he wasn't alone on the island. He knew about Ellie, probably from Leroy. That weasel would sell out his own mother. Anyway, I just wanted to keep my family safe."

The Stony Pointers found out that a rescue group was going to capture all of the dogs from Fuller's Island and find them all good homes. Even though they were bred for violence, the "devil dogs" were a loyal, dependable breed.

Ian and Annie also heard from the veterinarian to whom they had taken the heroic dog shot in the melee. The animal would make a full recovery, they were assured, and the vet himself had decided to adopt him.

On their last night before the drive home, Annie was packing when she heard a soft tap at the door. She opened it to find Ian standing in the hall. "May I come in?" he asked.

"Of course," Annie said, stepping back.

Ian looked around the clean, but plain, motel room. "It doesn't really have the charm of the Preacher's Rest," he said.

"No, but none of us have disappeared yet," Annie said.

Ian looked at her. "These mysteries of yours scare me, Annie."

"This one wasn't totally mine," she said.

He sighed. "I used to think I could talk you into being safe, but that's not really going to happen, is it?"

"I don't go looking for trouble," she said.

He nodded, stepping closer to her. "But you don't run from it either, and once you get hold of something, you won't let go."

Annie raised a shoulder in a half-shrug. "I can't change who I am."

Ian reached out and gently lifted a strand of Annie's blond hair away from her face. "How do I keep you safe?"

"You don't," she said. "It's not your job."

"Maybe I'd like it to be," Ian said.

Annie cleared her throat and took a step back. "Ian, I'm not looking for someone to look after me. I can look after myself."

"So there's no place for me?" Ian asked.

Annie smiled a little. "I didn't say that."

He took a step closer to her again and opened his mouth to say something when a knock at the door made them both jump. Annie slipped around Ian and opened the door. Jim and Alice stood in the doorway.

"Ah, the mayor's here too," Jim said cheerfully. "Alice and I wanted to see if anyone wanted to ride back to Stony Point in our car."

"Why? Did you think you might find some other near-death experience to take Annie and Alice on between here and Stony Point?" Ian asked.

Jim raised an eyebrow but just said, "You never know what we might find, mayor."

"You could have gotten Alice killed," Ian said. "And Annie too."

"I didn't drive Annie to South Carolina. Some other guy did," Jim said. "Oh, right, it was you."

"Hey, now," Alice said, stepping between them and slipping an arm through Jim's. "We saved those dogs from a horrible future, broke up a dogfighting ring, and freed a town from fear. We're heroes here. It all worked out for the best."

"This time," Ian said. "What happens next time?"

"I don't know," Alice said. "But I wouldn't miss it for the world. How about you, Annie?"

Annie looked between her friends. "Well, I could do without the swamp stench. I had to throw away two pairs of shoes." Then she smiled. "But it was exciting. And we helped people." She turned a mischievous glance toward Alice. "Those bad guys would have gotten away with it … ."

"If it hadn't been for us meddling kids," Alice finished before bursting into laughter.

Ian moaned and shook his head. Annie felt the last bit of tension fade from the room, and she looked at all her friends fondly. It was wonderful having everything back to normal. At least until something else interesting turned up in the attic.